NYPD

Puzzle

NYPD Puzzle

A Puzzle Lady Mystery

Parnell Hall

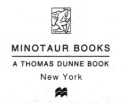

MINOTAUR BOOKS

A THOMAS DUNNE BOOK

New York

This is a work of fiction. All of the characters, organizations, and events portrayed in this novel are either products of the author's imagination or are used fictitiously.

A THOMAS DUNNE BOOK FOR MINOTAUR BOOKS.
An imprint of St. Martin's Publishing Group.

www.thomasdunnebooks.com
www.minotaurbooks.com

Library of Congress Cataloging-in-Publication Data

Hall, Parnell.
NYPD puzzle : a Puzzle Lady mystery / Parnell Hall. — First edition.
   p.   cm.
"A Thomas Dunne Book."
ISBN 978-1-250-02715-3 (hardcover)
ISBN 978-1-250-02716-0 (e-book)
1. Felton, Cora (Fictitious character)—Fiction.   2. Women detectives—Fiction.   3. Older women—Fiction.   4. Puzzles—Fiction.   5. Murder—Investigation—Fiction   6. Police—New York (State)—New York—Fiction.   I. Title.   II. Title.
PS3558.A37327N97 2014
813'.54—dc23

2013032461

Minotaur books may be purchased for educational, business, or promotional use. For information on bulk purchases, please contact Macmillan Corporate and Premium Sales Department at 1-800-221-7945, extension 5442, or write specialmarkets@macmillan.com.

First Edition: January 2014

10 9 8 7 6 5 4 3 2 1

For the NYPD

An NYPD Appreciation

On behalf of the NYPD, I would like to thank the following people for helping catch the killer. That may seem strange, since these people actually provided the puzzles used by the killer, but I think we can all agree they were merely setting the killer up.

At any rate, I would like to thank *New York Times* crossword puzzle editor Will Shortz for constructing the sudoku puzzles, frequent *New York Times* contributor Fred Piscop for constructing the crossword puzzles, and American Crossword Puzzle Tournament champion Ellen Ripstein for editing them. Without the help of these three experts, the killer never would have been caught.

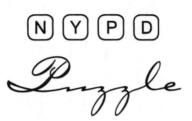

NYPD

Puzzle

Chapter 1

"Want a job?"

Cora Felton eyed Becky Baldwin suspiciously. "What kind of job?"

"A little detective work?"

"Does it involve blackmail?"

"No."

"Does it involve my ex-husband?"

"Which one?"

Cora rounded her lips, pointed at Becky. "Oooh. Nice shot. You are really getting quite accomplished. It's hard to believe you're only sixteen."

Becky was in her late twenties; she only *looked* sixteen. Her long blond hair, angel face, and willowy figure belied the fact that she was an accomplished trial lawyer who deserved a wider practice. The only thing that held her back was the fact that Baker-haven, Connecticut, had virtually no crime, aside from the occasional murder.

"Yeah, yeah," Becky said. "And I could have had a wonderful career as an attorney if I only had the gumption to leave town."

"Why don't you?"

"I don't want to work for a firm. I want to work for myself."

"Yeah, but if there *is* no work—"

"There's work. I have a case. You want in?"

"Is there a crossword puzzle involved?"

"You are the most suspicious person I ever met."

"That's an evasion."

Cora despised crossword puzzles, a rather unfortunate situation for the nationally famous Puzzle Lady, whose benevolent, grandmotherly face appeared on a syndicated daily crossword puzzle and who hawked breakfast cereal to school children on television. She hated crosswords because she couldn't do them. She was, in fact, a fraud, fronting for her niece. Sherry Carter originally dreamed up the idea as a means of hiding from her abusive ex-husband. Happily, that was no longer necessary; still, revealing to the puzzle-solving, breakfast-eating general population that the lovable icon they had been revering for years was actually the cruciverbal Milli Vanilli was not an option.

"There are no puzzles involved," Becky promised.

"Or ex-husbands?"

"Your ex-husband Melvin is not involved," Becky said. "As for the rest, I cannot be expected to keep track of all the men you might have married."

"I haven't married anyone in years," Cora said.

"Really? Are you still seeing Barney Nathan?"

"He went back to his wife," Cora said, not without a tinge of regret. Her affair with the married doctor had been her only serious entanglement in years. "I thought you knew that."

Becky smiled. "Actually, I did."

"Oooh," Cora said. "The bitchy barb. Snidely done. I like that."

"Thank you. Will you take the job?"

"Going to tell me who the client is?"

"Sure."

"Well, that's a switch. Lately you've been holding out on me, keeping me in the dark, treating me as a second-class citizen."

"Not this time."

"I'm glad to hear it. What do you want me to do?"

"That's what I'd like to know."

Cora frowned. "I beg your pardon?"

"We're meeting the client tomorrow. Assuming you're in."

"You haven't met the client?"

"I've talked to him on the phone."

"What did he want?"

"To meet me tomorrow."

"If I killed you, it would be justifiable homicide. *Why* does the client want to meet you tomorrow?"

"That's the beauty of the whole thing. I have no idea."

"Then how do you know you need me?"

"I'm psychic."

"Becky."

"I'm meeting the client tomorrow. I have no idea why. I want you there."

"Why?"

"I want a witness."

"That makes no sense. You can't have a confidential communication in the presence of a third person. You're a lawyer, you know that."

"I may not want to have a confidential communication."

"With your client?"

"He's not my client until I say so."

"He hasn't hired you yet?"

"He thinks he has."

"That's not the point," Cora said. "The point is, if he hasn't hired you, he isn't paying me."

"When he hires me, he will."

"And if he doesn't hire you, I don't get paid."

"You'll get paid."

"How?"

"*I'll* pay you."

Cora looked at her skeptically. "You'll pay me to sit in on an interview with your client?"

"That's right."

"I've already pointed out why that's a dumb idea. And you still want to do it. Let me see if I can figure out why."

Cora whipped out a pack of cigarettes.

"You can't smoke in here."

"I can if I'm doing a job and not getting paid."

"You'll get paid."

"Interesting," Cora mused. "Why would you pay me money just to come to your office? Ah! That's it! The meeting is not in your office."

"No."

"Where is the meeting?"

"In New York City."

Cora grinned. "Where in New York City?"

"Manhattan, actually."

"That's not what I meant. Are you meeting the client in his office at work?"

"No."

"You're meeting the client in his apartment."

"Actually—"

"In the apartment he shares with his wife who isn't home."

"No, I believe he's a bachelor."

"And you're meeting him in his bachelor apartment?"

"Actually, it's a penthouse."

"Ah! Of course! And what wonderful connotations that has—thank you, Bob Guccione."

"Is that a problem?"

"Oh, why should that be a problem?" Cora said ironically. "Let me see if I understand this: A young man is attempting to lure you up to his apartment with the offer of a job. You want me along, not for my keen insight, my astute judgment of character, or my impressive detective skills. You want me along because I'm tough as nails and have a gun in my purse."

"So?" Becky said. "What if I do?"

Cora smiled. "I like that."

Jennifer toddled across the lawn and wrapped her muddy arms around Cora's leg.

"Sherry," Cora protested. "Look what she's doing."

Sherry Carter, lounging in a lawn chair, said, "You wanted her to walk."

"I wanted her to walk *around*. I didn't want her to walk around *me.*"

Sherry wasn't impressed. "You can drop the gruff-aunt act. You know you love her."

"I'd love her more if she were holding onto *your* leg."

A car came up the driveway.

"Oh, look, it's Daddy," Sherry said.

Jennifer shrieked, "Daddy!" and took off across the lawn.

"What are you trying to do, teach her to run in front of cars?" Cora said.

"Relax. By the time she gets to the driveway, Aaron could have gone to the store and back."

Jennifer was indeed making rather slow progress, but not for want of trying. She would rush forward, fall on her face, pick herself up again, and repeat, having gained, if not wisdom, at least another fresh layer of dirt.

Aaron got out of the car to meet her. The young reporter wore a sports shirt, open at the neck. His clean khaki pants seemed an excellent target.

He held out his arms. "Come to Daddy!"

"You don't know what you're asking," Cora warned.

"He knows what he's asking," Sherry said. "He's asking me to do a laundry."

Jennifer fell into Daddy's arms. He lifted her up, spun her around.

"Don't get her dizzy," Cora said.

"You're worse than a mother hen," Sherry told her.

"She's just jealous," Aaron said. "You want me to spin you, Cora?"

"Just try it, buster."

"Cora got a job," Sherry said.

"Oh?"

"Becky Baldwin's chaperone."

"Bodyguard," Cora said.

"If you say so."

"Chaperones don't carry guns."

Aaron walked over to them, bouncing the baby on his hip. "What are you talking about?"

Cora filled him in on her assignment for Becky Baldwin.

"Sounds like fun," Aaron said.

"Fun? How can it possibly be fun?"

"It's in New York. Your appointment's in the afternoon, isn't it? Why don't you get theater tickets?"

"Are you suggesting I take Becky Baldwin to the theater?"

"Sure. Take her to *The Book of Mormon*."

"I don't date women."

"Like that's the only problem," Sherry said. "You can't get tickets to *The Book of Mormon*."

"Sure you can."

"Not on the same day."

"Hey, I'm a reporter. Let me see what I can do."

"You're going to get press passes?" Cora said. "I am not writing a damn review."

A car turned into the driveway.

"What is this, a convention?"

"It's Chief Harper," Sherry said. "I wonder what he wants."

Chief Harper pulled up behind Aaron and got out of the car. The chief had on his relaxed, friendly face, the one he wore in between cases, particularly cases involving Cora Felton. Cora had assisted the chief in a number of investigations, and while he appreciated her help, she exasperated him no end by evading direct questions, usually because she had something to conceal.

"Hi, Chief," Cora said. "Come to see my grandniece?"

Chief Harper belatedly took note of the baby. He leaned in, said, "Well, now, she is cute, isn't she?"

Jennifer tried to grab his tie.

He took a prudent step backwards. "And quick, too."

"Good work, Chief. We're trying to teach her to keep away from cops."

"A result of your Woodstock days, no doubt."

"Woodstock? Wouldn't know, Chief. I was a toddler then myself." She cocked her head. "So, who died?"

"What do you mean?"

"You're here because you got a murder and you want me to solve it."

"No one died."

"That's a shame. It's a result of people living too long. Social Security's going to run out long before I get there."

"You're in an awfully good mood."

"Why shouldn't I be? I haven't done anything. So, whatever happened, it's not my fault."

"I never said it was."

"Maybe not. I always assume you suspect me of something until you prove otherwise."

"Good Lord," Sherry said. "Are you two going to keep sparring or are you going to tell her what you want?"

"Hey, who asked your opinion?" Cora said.

"Don't you want to find out what's up?"

"Well, if you'd stop interrupting the man, maybe he'd tell me."

"Interrupting?"

Aaron Grant grinned at Chief Harper. "I think they've forgotten about you."

"Probably just as well."

"What did you want, anyway?"

"I should probably tell Cora."

Cora broke off from arguing with her niece. "Go ahead, lay it on me, Chief. You haven't got a puzzle you want me to solve, have you?"

"No, I don't. I've got a case that has me puzzled, though."

"Your default position."

"Hey."

"What you got?"

"I had a break-in last week."

"And you're just getting to it now?"

"Ha ha. The fact is, I can't make any headway." Harper pointed at Aaron. "And I'd rather not see an editorial about it."

"Maybe there's nowhere to get," Cora said.

"Doors don't break themselves. Someone jimmied this one with a crowbar."

"What was taken?"

"Nothing."

"Nothing?"

"There's nothing to take."

"Whoa. Time out, Chief. I think you left out a main detail of the story. Whose house is this?"

"It's not a private home."

"It was a store?"

"No."

"You gonna make me play Twenty Questions? Come on, Chief. What was broken into?"

"The town hall."

Chief Harper was unusually quiet on the ride to town.

"Cheer up, Chief. This is not the crime of the century."

"Yeah, I know."

"What's bugging you?"

"I don't know. He sighed. "We got this case, and we'll solve it or we won't solve it, just business as usual. And then we'll chalk it up and go on to the next."

"Good Lord. What brought this on?"

"I don't know. I'm just starting to feel old."

"Join the club. You're a little late getting there, but don't worry, you'll fit right in."

"Yeah."

"What's the matter?"

Harper grimaced. "I had to testify at Stuart Tanner's parole hearing last month."

"Who?"

"Our first case. The girl in the cemetery."

"What about it?"

Solving that murder had been the beginning of Chief Harper and Cora's collaboration, though the chief hadn't known it at the time. They'd been solving crimes ever since.

"That was Stuart Tanner. He's up for parole."

"*What?*"

"Exactly."

"He was convicted of murder! Three counts!"

"Yeah. He got twenty-five to life."

"I can do the math. If he's not dead, he's got a few years to go."

"Yeah," Harper said in disgust. "If twenty-five to life *meant* twenty-five to life. It *ought* to mean he's there for life, unless he's such a *wonderful* individual that sometime after he's served twenty-five years and before he's dead, a parole board *could* consider releasing him early. But they don't have to *do* it. They shouldn't have to grant him parole unless *they* can prove he doesn't deserve it. They should have the right to keep him until *he* proves he deserves to get *out*. Even then, it should be their decision."

"Whoa, Chief. Let's not go off on a tangent. You're frustrated with the system. I get that. You've strayed from the main point. Twenty-five to life. I may be a little dotty myself, but if it's been twenty-five years since I moved to Bakerhaven, I'm really losing it."

"That's what I was saying. Twenty-five to life should mean twenty-five to life. But, no, the son of a bitch can apply for parole after twelve."

"It's been *that* long?"

"See what I mean?"

"So the son of a bitch could get out?"

Harper smiled grimly. "Not after what *I* told the parole board."

Cora lapsed into silence. Damn. Now *she* felt old.

The Bakerhaven town hall, like most of the other buildings in town, was white with black shutters. Of course it was larger than most, with wide front steps and a double door. Harper drove around to the parking lot in the back.

Cora inspected the back door. "The lock's been replaced."

"Yes, it has. But you can still see the damage."

"Yes. You think it was a crowbar?"

"Some sort of pry bar. Or a very large screwdriver."

"Okay, let's go inside."

Cora came down off the back steps.

"We can go in this way." Harper jerked a ring of keys out of his pocket.

"You have the key to town hall?"

"One of the perks of the job."

They went inside, found themselves in a small back hallway. To the right was the town meeting hall. To the left were the town offices.

"Okay," Cora said. "What's there to steal?"

"Like I said, nothing."

"There's no money?"

"No."

"What about my taxes?"

"Pays my salary."

"And there's nothing left over? I'm not the only one paying tax, you know."

"You pay your taxes in cash?"

"I pay my taxes in blood." Cora looked around. "Okay, so once he got inside, where did he go?"

"I have no idea."

"No door was left open? Nothing was disturbed?"

"If there was, I'd have an idea."

"Did you ask?"

Harper gave her a look.

Cora pushed open the door and found herself in the front of the town hall assembly. Cora had been in the front of the room before; she had just never come in the back door. An audience of chairs faced her. A lectern on the small stage to the right was where she had often held forth.

"You sure you publicized this meeting, Chief? Attendance is poor."

"Anytime you're through clowning around."

"I assume nothing was taken from the meeting room. There *is* nothing in the meeting room, is there?"

"As long as the lectern's still there."

Cora closed the door, checked out the corridor. Four doors with frosted glass panels led off to the left. One said TOWN CLERK. One said TAX ASSESSOR. The other two were farther down the hall.

Cora pushed through the door marked TOWN CLERK. All four doors led to the same room. A woman with curly red hair and green eyes behind wire-rimmed glasses sat at a desk. Cora wondered if she dyed her hair. The woman was not much younger than she was.

There was no nameplate on the woman's desk, which was too bad. Cora recognized her from Cushman's Bake Shop, but had no idea who she was.

"Excuse me, Mae," Harper said, solving half the problem. "You got a minute?"

Mae put down her pen, folded her hands, straightened in her chair, and looked up at the chief. "Certainly," she said. The woman had an air of pedantic efficiency about her. She managed to give the impression of being terribly put-upon while cooperating fully.

Cora wanted to kick her.

"The problem here," Harper said, "is we can't figure out what there is here to steal. Can you think of anything anyone would want?"

Mae put up her hand. "As I told you, I don't keep anything valuable in the office."

"I wondered if you'd thought of anything."

"If I had, I would have told you."

"Yes, of course," Harper said. "There's no money kept here?"

"That would be something of value."

"There's no personal items you might leave overnight?"

Mae explained as to a small child. "No. I don't *keep* personal items in the office."

"And the night of the break-in. You're sure you didn't leave anything out someone might have taken?"

Mae drew herself up even straighter. She could not have been more rigid had she had a metal rod in her backside, which Cora thought was entirely possible. "I assure you, none of this is my fault."

Chief Harper put up his hands in a placating manner. "No one's accusing you of anything."

"I wouldn't be too sure of that," Cora said.

Mae's mouth dropped open.

"If anything's missing, that would be the responsibility of the person in charge," Cora said. "I would assume that's you. Don't worry. We can help you. When's the last time you took inventory?"

"Inventory?"

"Yeah. Took out your files, checked that everything was logged accurately."

"Everything *is* logged accurately."

"Glad to hear it. When's the last time you checked?"

Mae blinked.

"Don't worry," Cora said. "Most likely it's not your fault, it's the tax assessor."

She blinked again.

"Well?"

"I'm the tax assessor."

"Interesting. I've been meaning to talk to you about my property tax. I suppose it's not the time. What sort of records do you keep that someone might want to have access to?"

"It's a public office. Everyone has access to the records."

"Well, that's not exactly true, is it?" Cora said. "You don't have people in here all day pawing through your files. Don't they have to *request* the information and *you* go through your files?"

"Yes, of course."

"Well, let's take a look."

"You're not going through my files."

"Why? Is anything wrong with your files?"

"Absolutely not."

"You checked them all? You must have logged a lot of over-time. That's a lot of files."

"I already told Chief Harper."

"Now you can tell me."

"The questions are the same, no matter who asks them."

"Then the answers should be the same. That will make it easy."

"Chief Harper is the chief of police."

"Yes, he is. Astute of you to notice."

The argument might have continued, had Chief Harper not jumped in and managed to herd Cora out the door.

"Why'd you stop me, Chief? I had her on the ropes."

"Yes, you did. And if my object had been to put the town clerk in her place, I would have let you continue. I was hoping to solve a crime."

Cora started to flare up, but saw the chief's eyes twinkling in amusement. She bit off her angry retort, sidespied up at him imp-ishly.

"Spoilsport."

Chapter

4

Cora came out of Cushman's Bake Shop and bumped into Barney Nathan. As always, the little doctor was wearing his red bow tie. He was impeccably dressed, but his face was drawn, and he looked more harried than usual, even on those occasions when his medical competence was questioned on the witness stand.

"Hi, Barney."

"Oh. Hi," Barney said. He looked very uncomfortable.

"So, how you been?"

"I, eh . . ."

Cora smiled. "No good at this, are you, Barney?"

"Good at what?"

"Post-breakup confrontations. You haven't had much practice."

"You're not making it easy."

"Yes, I am. Have I tried to rip your face off? Have I burst into tears and made a public scene?"

Barney looked nervous at the thought. "You wouldn't do that."

"You're speaking from your vast experience?"

"Cora."

"How's your wife?"

Barney took a breath. "I really must be going."

"Yes. You have patients this morning."

"Yes."

"Amazing you got away."

"I had a break in my schedule."

"A break between patients? Wow. I've never heard that before. A doctor with a break between patients. Usually a doctor's patients tend to fill the time allowed, even if there's a cancellation. Don't you double- or triple-book? Most doctors do. You sign in at the front desk and find out two other patients have signed in for the exact same time. So, you're back with your wife. How much did you have to grovel?"

Barney looked hurt.

"Oh, don't make those sad doe-eyes at me. Poor little boy wronged. Taken advantage of by the wicked, scheming hussy."

A woman on her way into Cushman's Bake Shop turned her head.

"I thought you weren't going to make a public display," Barney said.

"You call this a public display? This is an amiable chat. Trust me, if I make a public display, you'll know it. Just ask Melvin."

"I'm not your ex-husband."

"I'm glad to hear it. Marrying you would have voided my alimony. Plus making you a bigamist. Much better this way."

"Well, I must get back."

"When?"

"Huh?"

"When do you have to get back? You were on your way *into* Cushman's Bake Shop. Aren't you going to get your coffee?"

"Oh."

Cora grinned. "You don't have a break between patients, do you? You were checking out the bakery because you know I hang out there. You *wanted* to run into me. I think that's sweet. But that's one of those fantasies plays much better in your head. When it actually happens, you don't know what to do. Relax. You're not alone. Most men don't. So, you going to get your coffee or not?"

Barney nodded stiffly, turned, and walked away.

Cora watched him go with mixed emotions. Damn the son of a bitch. It was hard enough dealing with an ex-lover who knew the ropes. But a babe in the wilderness was annoying, even if he was sweet.

Especially if he was sweet.

5

Becky Baldwin piloted Cora's red Toyota down the Saw Mill River Parkway toward New York.

"Got your gun?" Becky said.

Cora reached into her floppy drawstring purse and whipped out a revolver.

"Hey, don't point that thing at me! I didn't ask to see it, I just asked if you had it."

"Relax," Cora said. She snapped the cylinder open, gave it a spin. It was fully loaded, a bullet in every chamber. She knew it would be. Cora always cleaned and reloaded her gun after target practice. It was one of the things her ex-husband Melvin had taught her. Still, she dumped all the bullets out into her hand to make sure none were fired. Satisfied, she reloaded the cylinder, flipped it shut with an expert flick of the wrist.

"You think that reassures me, or are you just showing off?" Becky said.

"I'm just being careful. Isn't that what you lawyers do, cross the *t*'s and dot the *i*'s wearing a belt and suspenders?"

"I never wear a belt and suspenders," Becky said.

"Even in that faux-fireman outfit you wore for that calendar?"

"I understand," Becky said. "You're sniping at me to cover your fear of Alzheimer's that makes you doubt your memory."

"Yeah," Cora said. "Like when Chief Harper told me about Stuart Tanner."

"Who?"

"You don't know? That makes me feel better. That was the killer we put away, first case I worked on. Guy's been in so long, he came up for parole."

"He's getting paroled?"

"No, but he's eligible. Which is depressing. It's been so long, I barely remember him. It's reassuring you don't remember him either."

"Actually, that was before I came back to town."

"Are you sure?"

"You were here when I got here. Probating that old lady's estate."

"Oh, yeah." Cora was vague on those events, but that was back in the days when she was drinking heavily, so her lack of memory was not necessarily due to age.

She did recall one detail. "Wasn't that when you were riding around on the back of some young hooligan's motorcycle?"

"He was a very nice young man."

"He was a murder suspect."

"He wasn't guilty."

"You didn't know it at the time."

Becky pouted. "Why are you lashing out at me?"

"I wasn't lashing out. I was replying in kind."

"Replying to what? I wasn't attacking you."

Cora shrugged. "Things haven't been the same between us. Ever since Barney Nathan."

Becky Baldwin's eyes widened. "You did *not* steal Barney Nathan away from me. I was never *involved* with Barney Nathan."

"That's not what I hear."

"Of course not," Becky said sarcastically. "After you spread all those rumors about me."

"What rumors? I said nothing but the unvarnished truth. Did Barney Nathan ask you out on a date?"

"That's not the point."

"How is that not the point? It's not a lie to say he asked you out on a date if he asked you out on a date."

"I didn't go."

"I never said you did."

Becky took a breath. "Look. I'm an attorney. I could cross-examine you and pin you down, but I don't want to. You know and I know you manipulated your statements in order to give the *impression* that I was having an affair with Barney Nathan."

"Now you're just being paranoid."

"His wife *slapped* me."

"See? That probably did more to fuel the rumors than anything *I* ever did."

"She slapped me *because* you manipulated the truth about Barney and me."

"How could I do that?"

"I don't know how you did, but you did. I don't know *why* you did, either. It's like you get some wicked thrill out of messing with people."

"You think I do that?"

"I *know* you do that."

"Then why ask?"

Becky lapsed into silence. After a few minutes she said, "I don't see why I have to drive."

"You wanted to use my car."

"For a long trip, it's nicer than my car."

"Exactly."

"What do you mean, exactly?"

"If you want to use my car, you can drive. A cooperative effort. I provide the car, you provide the driver."

Becky refrained from comment.

"What's the guy's name?" Cora asked.

"Charles Kessington."

"*Sir* Charles Kessington?"

"Why do you say that?"

"Sounds like royalty, doesn't it?"

"You think you're protecting me from some English lord?"

"They can get frisky. Droit du seigneur and all that."

"He's not British. He's American."

"How do you know?"

"I talked to him."

"You met him?"

"On the phone. I talked to him on the phone."

"I'm not sure all Englishmen have an accent."

"Stop it."

"Stop what?"

"You're just trying to humor me so I'll forget what you did."

"Oh, come on, Becky. After all I've done for you. You're gonna harp on one little thing?"

"See? I knew it."

"Knew what?"

"I wondered how long it would take before you got to that."

"Got to what?"

"All you've done for me."

Cora had helped Becky out of a tricky situation involving blackmail that could have scuttled her law practice. It had not been easy. Several legal statutes had to be broken.

"Becky, we're friends. What kind of a friendship is it if we can't kid each other over men? You're ridiculously young. You don't know what it's like for a woman of my age just to play in your ballpark."

Becky got off the highway at Seventy-ninth Street, went through Central Park at Eighty-first.

"Where we going?" Cora said.

"Eighty-fifth and Madison."

"Good. There's meters on Madison."

"How long are they for?"

"An hour."

"That's no good. I don't know how long this is going to take. We'll have to put it in a garage."

"You don't want a garage up here."

"Why not?"

"We want to park near the Theater District, so we can get the car after the show."

Aaron had succeeded in getting them tickets to *The Book of Mormon*. Cora was looking forward to it.

"We'll get another garage down there."

"That's going to be expensive."

"So? The client's paying for it."

"I thought he wasn't your client yet."

"He's gonna be. I need the work."

Becky pulled into a garage on Eighty-fourth Street.

Cora's mouth fell open at the prices. "My God, it would be cheaper just to leave it here and buy a new car."

"Relax," Becky told her. She took the ticket from the parking attendant and surrendered the car keys.

"How do you want to play this?" Cora said.

"What do you mean, 'play this'? It's perfectly straightforward. I'm here for a business meeting."

"How are you going to explain an armed bodyguard?"

"I don't have to explain anything. Who's gonna ask me?"

"The doorman will ask who's calling."

"I'll tell him 'Becky Baldwin to see Mr. Kessington.'"

"He's not going to ask my name?"

"Why would he?"

"Seems rather inefficient to me. Saying Becky Baldwin is there to see him will be entirely misleading."

"I certainly hope so," Becky said.

They went in the building, where a uniformed doorman sat behind a desk. "May I help you?" he said.

"Becky Baldwin to see Mr. Kessington."

"One moment, please." The doorman picked up a house phone, punched in a number. "A Miss Becky Baldwin to see you." He hung up the phone, said, "Go right on up. Apartment P-Two."

"P-Two?"

"That's the penthouse."

"Of course."

Cora followed Becky into the elevator. Becky pushed P. "P-two," Cora said.

"So?"

"There's two penthouses. It's not like he's got the whole top floor."

Becky gave her a look.

"I'm just saying. If you're thinking of marrying the guy."

"I wasn't."

"Well, if you were, he's not as rich as you thought. Because there's two penthouses."

Actually, there were three. Becky and Cora emerged from the elevator to find a longer corridor than they might have expected, with three doors scattered around. Defying logic, P3 was directly in front of them, P1 was to the right, P2 was to the left.

"Confusing," Cora said. "I'm sure if you live here long enough, you get used to it."

"Shh."

"I wonder if this was originally one penthouse and they cut it up."

"Shut up."

Becky went down the hall, rang the bell of P2.

They waited, but no one came to the door.

"He must not have heard you," Cora said.

"He knows we're coming. He picked up the phone."

"He knows *you're* coming," Cora said. "Ring him again."

Becky pushed the button. They could hear the chime ringing inside. Again there was no answer.

"He's gotta be there," Cora said.

Cora barged in front of Becky, banged on the door.

It opened.

Just an inch, but enough to show it wasn't locked.

"There you go," Cora said. "He got tied up on the phone and left the door open for us." She pushed the door open, walked in.

The foyer was lavishly decorated with a Persian rug, freestanding statuary, and an ornate umbrella stand and coatrack, superfluous on a warm sunny day.

Cora didn't waste time taking it in. She marched straight through the foyer and the wide double doors into a living room with mahogany walls, brass fixtures, velvet couches, leather chairs, and a marble mantelpiece over an exceptionally wide hearth.

The body of a well-dressed young man lay in front of the fireplace. Blood was seeping from a wound in his forehead.

There was a crossword puzzle on his chest.

Across

1 Greet the villain
5 Gyro bread
9 Sleeper, diner, etc.
13 Bubbly name
14 Visibly frightened
15 Lieutenant-to-be
16 Start of a message
18 Appliance brand
19 Cold War follower
20 Independence Hall figure
21 Fenway abbr.
22 More desirable, in a way
24 Trimmed back
27 More of the message
31 In crowd
32 Nobel Peace Prize city
33 Plug away
34 Coffeehouse jar input
35 Glossy fabrics
38 32-Across loc.

(continued)

(continued)

39 Boater's hazard
41 "Confound it!"
42 Demagnetize, maybe
44 Still more of the message
46 Social customs
47 Farm equipment name
48 Bad start?
49 Ace location?
52 Defeats, like Joey Chestnut
56 "M" star
57 End of the message
59 Windows typeface
60 Wile E. Coyote's supplier
61 Hosiery shade
62 Get naked
63 Hammered on a slant
64 Judgment Day

Down

1 Flush, e.g.
2 Therapist's words
3 Margin marking
4 Auxiliary action
5 Conflict enders
6 Club Med locale
7 T-giving day
8 Roll-call call
9 Mustangs' counterparts
10 "__ had 'em"

11 French politico Coty
12 Phone key
15 Sitcom star Drew
17 Battery terminals
20 Ozone-unfriendly gas
22 Second-stringer
23 Francis of "What's My Line?"
24 __ dish (lab vessel)
25 Xenophobe's fear
26 Approach readiness
27 Windbag's output
28 Of an arm bone
29 Unwelcome grab
30 Shrek and Fiona, for two
36 Campaign expenditure
37 Arab, e.g.
40 FDIC part
43 Pinkish hue
45 Party hearty
48 Like cell phones in church, hopefully
49 Reaction to a 29-Down, perhaps
50 Griot's collection
51 Sal's canal
52 Treater's words
53 Not pizzicato
54 Mower name
55 Done laps, maybe
57 Eliot's Grizabella, e.g.
58 Tree-hugger's prefix

Chapter

6

Cora was furious.

"I don't believe it!" she stormed. "Of all the luck! The best part of getting out of Bakerhaven was not having to be the Puzzle Lady. So what do I find? A goddamned crossword puzzle!"

"There's also a corpse."

"That I can handle. I don't mind corpses. I'm good with corpses. Plus the fact the guy's dead makes keeping him from molesting you a lot easier. Strictly a win–win. But, oh, no. The killer's got to leave a crossword puzzle."

"What does it say?"

"How the hell should I know?"

"Oh. That's right." Becky was one of the few people who knew Cora couldn't solve crossword puzzles. She just didn't know she couldn't construct them either.

Becky started for the phone.

"What are you doing?"

"Calling the police."

"What, are you nuts? I thought you were a lawyer. This is a crime scene and you're going to touch the phone?"

"Right." Becky whipped out her cell phone.

Cora grabbed her arm. "Let's not be hasty."

"What?"

"You haven't thought this through. We checked in at the front desk. You gave your right name."

"That's why we have to call."

"Yeah, but the doorman called upstairs. This guy took the call. You know what that means. He was killed while we were coming up in the elevator."

"You mean the killer's still here?"

"Hell no. The killer heard the call. He knew we were coming up. He killed the guy and split. Which makes it very bad. As far as the doorman is concerned, we're the ones who killed him."

"Don't be stupid."

"Why is that stupid?"

"What did we shoot him with? Your gun hasn't been fired, has it?"

"No."

"There you are."

"We could have ditched the weapon."

"How?"

"I don't know. Thrown it out the window. Dropped it down the garbage chute. Assuming it's not on the floor somewhere. For all we know, the killer kicked it under the couch."

"We could prove we didn't fire it with a paraffin test."

"We could if we go to court. When we get arrested and booked, it's not going to cheer me knowing you can get the charges kicked six months down the road."

"Sorry, Cora. You're not going to kid me out of it."

"And we don't even know this is Kessington. Shouldn't we at least ID the guy so we don't sound like a couple of jerks?"

"I don't think image is our primary problem." Becky shook her head. "Sorry." She flipped the cell phone open.

"What was that?" Cora said.

"What?"

"I heard something."

"Heard what?"

"I don't know. If I did, I wouldn't be asking."

"You're just stalling."

"There!" Cora pointed. "You hear that?"

"No."

A floorboard creaked.

"Yes," Becky amended. She dropped her voice to a whisper. "It's the killer! You think he knows we're here?"

"Unless he's deaf," Cora said.

"If he heard us, why wouldn't he leave?"

"Maybe he's one of those guys gets off on danger."

"All the more reason to call the cops."

"Yeah. Like they're gonna get here in time to save us." Cora reached in her purse, pulled out her gun.

"What are you doing?"

"I don't know about you, but I'm not going quietly. Somebody shot this guy. If it's the guy in the bedroom, he's got a gun and he's not afraid to use it. Can you really see him letting us live?"

"We haven't seen his face. We don't know who he is."

"He's cornered in the bedroom. How's he going to get out without being seen?"

"I'm calling the cops."

"Fine. You do that."

Cora raised the gun, started for the bedroom.

"What are you doing?" Becky whispered.

Cora ignored her, reached the door, stepped through.

She was in a short hallway with several doors leading off it. The one at the end was open into what appeared to be a master bedroom. Cora tiptoed down the hallway. She flattened herself against the wall, peered in the door.

It was indeed the master bedroom, boasting a huge four-poster bed of solid wood that resembled an old sailing vessel more than a place to sleep.

A framed painting—which for all Cora knew might have been an original—lay on the bed. Above the headboard, where it had obviously hung, was a wall safe.

A man stood on the bed. His back was to Cora. He was working on the safe. He wore black slacks and a skintight black T-shirt. He was trim and athletic looking, but that was all Cora could tell. The man had a nylon stocking over his head.

It occurred to Cora that that answered the question of how he intended to get by them without being seen. She wondered if that meant he hadn't intended to kill them. It didn't matter now. The stocking was up around his forehead. The minute he turned around, Cora would see his face.

"All right," Cora said. "Put your hands in the air and turn around, nice and slow."

The man froze, his hands still on the combination dial. Then, slowly, he raised them up in front of his face. Just as his hands came level with his forehead, he grabbed the edge of the nylon stocking and jerked it down over his face. In the same motion he spun around and sprang sideways off the bed, diving into a somersault. He rolled over and came up with a gun in his hand. He brandished it wildly, ran for the open window, and, to Cora's astonishment, dived through.

From the *penthouse*?

Cora gawked in amazement.

The man's head popped up from beneath the windowsill. His gun swung in Cora's direction.

Cora fired.

The bullet whistled by his head and he took off.

Cora crept to the window, peered out.

He was gone!

A balcony ran along the side of the building and disappeared around the corner. The railing was low, the balcony narrow. Cora wasn't about to follow. But where did it lead? There must be a door, and—

Becky!

Cora sprinted for the living room, collided with Becky in the hall.

"I heard a shot!"

"That was me."

"You shot him?"

"I missed him."

"Where is he?"

"I don't know. I'm afraid he's in the apartment."

"What?"

"Get behind me!"

"Cora."

"I got a gun. You don't."

"Why'd you try to shoot him?"

"He tried to shoot me. I shot first."

"But—"

"Shut up. Just get behind me."

Cora poked her head into the living room, gun first. There was no one in sight. Cora wasn't convinced. "Stay down. Follow me."

"What do we do now?"

"We're leaving."

"We can't leave."

"We can't stay. There's a guy here with a gun."

Crouching, Cora stalked her way into the room.

The door flew open and two cops burst in, guns drawn. Whatever they'd been expecting, it wasn't Cora. The younger cop gawked. The older cop leveled his gun.

"All right, lady, hold it right there!"

Cora was furious.

"You idiots! The killer's getting away!"

One cop was impossibly young, with a chubby baby face. "Oh, I don't think so," he said, and laughed at his own joke.

"Not me, nimrod, the prowler. The thief. He could be hiding in the apartment."

"I doubt that." He snapped handcuffs on Cora's wrists.

Cora opened her mouth to tear him a new one.

"Shut up, Cora," Becky said. "As your attorney, I advise you to be quiet."

"You're a lawyer?" The young cop was immensely tickled. "Hey, Charlie. You hear that? She's a lawyer."

Charlie was stocky, bullnecked, and apparently humorless. He never cracked a smile. He rose from inspecting the body, looked Becky up and down. "She's a murder suspect, that's what she is." He spun Becky around, snapped on the cuffs.

"Oh, for goodness' sakes," Becky said.

"See?" Cora said. "Not so easy to keep quiet when it happens to you."

"Nothing's happening to me," Becky said irritably. "You're the suspect, I'm the attorney. He's just posturing."

"For Christ's sake," Cora said. "You really want to stand here bickering while some psychopath comes out of the kitchen, shoots us in the head? Believe me or don't believe me, but if you ever had *any* police training, try to recall the part about securing the premises."

Charlie nodded his head. "Check it out, Mark. I think I can handle these two."

"Wonderful," Cora said. "If he gets shot dead, would you be willing to entertain the thought that I didn't do it?"

"Mark can take care of himself."

"As long as no thinking's involved?"

"Shut up, Cora."

"Are you really a lawyer?"

"She's really a lawyer. You really a cop?"

"Cora!"

Cora took a breath, turned to Charlie. "Okay, if my lawyer were letting me talk, and if I were telling the truth, and if you were willing to listen, and if you checked out the bedroom and found the safe the killer was attempting to crack, you might want to check out the wide-open bedroom window just on the off chance an athletic killer in skintight black shirt and pants with a nylon stocking over his head escaped that way. If my lawyer were allowing me to talk, that's what I would advise."

The young cop named Mark came back. "Kitchen's clean."

"We're not interested in his housekeeping," Cora said. "What about the killer?"

Mark scowled. "That supposed to be funny?"

"Right, right," Cora said. "I forgot. You're the only one who can make the jokes."

"Check out the bedroom, Mark."

"Huh?"

"If the window's open, check if anyone could have gone out there."

"That what she says?"

"Uh-huh."

"You believe her?"

"Not for a second. Find me something proves her wrong."

Mark nodded, headed for the bedroom.

"Well, that's more like it," Cora said. "You mind keeping your gun ready in case he flushes anyone out?"

"Relax, lady."

"I'll relax when I'm dead. Which may be soon, if you don't get your gun out."

The cop came back from the bedroom. "No one there."

"You go out on the ledge?" Cora said.

"I told you, no one's there."

"Did you go out on the ledge?" his partner asked.

"Like hell. You have to be nuts to go out on the ledge."

"Or have just killed someone," Cora said. "Okay, Becky, do your stuff. Come up with some legal mumbo jumbo makes these flatfoots release us or haul us downtown before they get us killed."

They hauled them downtown.

Chapter

8

A uniformed cop ushered Cora into a small office, pointed to a chair in front of a cluttered desk, and went out. Cora was tempted to search the desk, not in the hope of finding a means of escape, but just for spite. It occurred to her she'd probably gotten into enough trouble for one day. She stifled the urge, contented herself with glancing around the office.

There was not much to see. Aside from a file cabinet and what appeared to be an ancient fax machine, it was remarkably unadorned.

A stocky man with a crew cut and a bulldog jaw came in with a file folder. His blue jacket was too large for him, as if a little boy had tried on his father's suit, remarkable considering his size. Without a word to Cora, he sat opposite her and flipped open the file.

"You Cora Felton?"

Cora was in no mood to cooperate. "That what it says there?" she said defiantly.

"That's right." He shrugged. "Doesn't mean you are, but it makes it entirely likely. You care to dispute the fact?"

"You the ADA?" Cora said. She tended to doubt it. The man had his shirt collar open and his tie pulled off to one side as if he were a newspaper reporter in some '40s noir movie about to bang out a story on an old Smith-Corona manual typewriter.

His nose crinkled as if he'd just smelled something foul. "No," he said shortly. "I'm Sergeant Crowley, Homicide."

"Oh," Cora said. Her expression matched that of the sergeant.

Sergeant Crowley frowned. "You *want* to see an ADA?"

"I haven't had much luck with cops."

"Oh?"

"The bozos who brought me in let the murderer get away. That's just for starters. They're lucky they didn't get shot."

"You almost shot them?"

"Don't be dumb. They're lucky the killer didn't shoot them while they were hassling me."

"You must admit they had some provocation. They respond to a report of shots fired, find you holding a gun."

"Well, if you're going to nitpick," Cora said.

The sergeant actually smiled. "Would you care to elaborate on that statement?"

"No."

"Because I'm not an ADA?"

"Because you're not listening. Once the two geniuses got it in their heads I'd committed the crime, they weren't interested in anything else."

"Again we come to the gun. Which I understand had been fired."

"Which was unlikely to be fired again, having been surrendered," Cora countered. "Which I certainly wouldn't have done if I hadn't mistakenly assumed two armed cops were going to be able to protect me from the killer."

The sergeant shrugged. "Be reasonable. Why should they suspect another killer?"

"Because I gave them a hint. I said, 'Hey, watch out for the killer.' "

He nodded. "I see. You assumed they were green at the game and had never encountered a criminal who suggested the crime had been committed by someone else."

"Oh, for Christ's sake," Cora said. "Could you speak English? Could you at least talk decent cop? You sound like you're practicing elocution lessons."

He grimaced. "Got me. Guess I'm a little intimidated. They told me you were that puzzle person."

Cora's face showed dismay. "Oh, for Christ's sake."

"It's true, isn't it? You're the Puzzle Lady person? You sell breakfast cereal on TV."

"You watch children's television?"

"Some of my detectives got young kids."

"I'm thrilled. You think they'll like it when they hear you're busting the Granville Grains Corn Toasties lady?"

"I was hoping that wouldn't happen. You seem to be leaving us little choice. If I didn't know better, I'd think you want to be arrested."

"Think again."

"Help me out, then. What were you doing in that apartment with a loaded gun?"

"This is the part where I'd like to have a lawyer."

"You have the right to an attorney."

"Glad you think so. My lawyer's locked up and they won't let me see her."

The sergeant consulted the chart. "Yeah. Arrested in the commission of a felony. Must be a nuisance when that happens."

"Aren't you enjoying this a little too much?"

"Well, it's certainly a change of pace from my standard routine. If it weren't for the dead man involved, this would be a pretty good day."

Cora sized up the situation. In spite of looking like a refugee from a chain gang, the sergeant appeared to have a sense of humor, and didn't seem to be treating her seriously as a murder suspect. Maybe he was actually a human being.

Cora gave him her most ingratiating smile. Had she been on television, the sale of Corn Toasties would have shown a considerable bump. "Sergeant, any way we could wrap this up? I got tickets for *The Book of Mormon.*"

The sergeant frowned. "What?"

Oh, dear. Maybe he wasn't a smart man playing dumb. Maybe he *was* dumb.

"I have theater tickets."

"Oh. Sort of a low priority, don't you think? Compared to a murder charge."

"Am I charged with murder?"

"You're not charged with anything. We're just talking here. Now, there's two ways this can go. You can cooperate and we can try to work things out. I'm not saying it'll happen, but it's probably your best shot. Or you can stand pat and demand to have a lawyer. And we can charge you and book you and you can get to see that ADA you were talking about."

"Is that a threat?"

"Good heavens, no. Just making a good faith attempt to clear things up."

"I think I'd rather hear a threat."

The sergeant sighed. "All right, lady. I'm trying to be nice. It clearly isn't working. Here's the situation: You can either answer my questions or you can go back in the holding cell while you think it over."

"See, that's a threat. Much easier, don't you think?"

The cop was not amused. He raised his head, bellowed, "Perkins!"

"Is that your safe word?" Cora said. "When the situation's out of hand and you're afraid you'll get hurt, you say 'Perkins.' "

The door opened and the uniformed cop stuck his head in. "Sir?"

"Miss Felton doesn't want to play nice. Why don't you take her back into the holding cell until she's arraigned?"

"Arraigned?" Cora said. "On what charge?"

"Well, that's something that the ADA you were talking about is going to come up with. Me, I'm just a dumb cop."

"Dumb like a fox," Cora said. "Okay, Perkins, cool your heels. Look, Sergeant, it's not that I like your company much, but you got the holding cell beat all to hell. Send your flunky away and let's give it another shot."

Perkins, who apparently didn't like being called a flunky, said, "You want me to handcuff her, Sergeant?"

"Not if you think you can handle her."

"Okay, lady, let's go."

"Hang on! Geez, you really know how to rub it in. You wanna talk, let's talk. And I will call this fine, upstanding officer anything he wants if he will just go away."

"That'll do, Perkins," Crowley said.

Perkins gave Cora the benefit of a cold, hard stare before going out and closing the door.

Cora watched him go. She turned back to find Sergeant Crowley looking at her expectantly.

"All right," Cora said. "I give up. You bluff better than I do."

"I wasn't bluffing."

"That's the basis of a good bluff. The fact that it isn't. You wanna talk, talk."

"You're the one wants to talk. What were you doing in the apartment of a man who got shot with a gun that had recently been fired?"

"Would that be a crime?"

"You're the one answering the questions."

"Yes, I am. But if you suspect me of a crime, I have the right to an attorney. That is not the right to hear you make clever remarks about how attorneys shouldn't get arrested. That is the right to have you produce my attorney so that I can make my statement without violating my constitutional rights. Please note I am not refusing to talk. I am merely attempting to make sure my rights are protected when I do."

Sergeant Crowley glared at her for a moment. "Perkins!" he bellowed again. Cora understood why there were no pictures on the walls. They never would have survived the vibrations.

The young officer must have been right outside. "Sergeant?" he said, popping in the door. He had a triumphant look on his face.

He was bound to be disappointed.

"Go to the women's lockup and bring me Miss Felton's lawyer."

"Yes, sir. And who would that be?" Perkins said.

"Are you gay?" Cora said.

Perkins's mouth fell open.

Sergeant Crowley blinked. "What?"

"If he's not gay, send him down to lockup, tell him to bring back anyone he wants." Cora smiled. "He'll pick the right one."

Becky was madder than a wet hen. Cora had never seen a wet hen, but she was sure Becky qualified. She came into the office in handcuffs. Her first words were, "Have they manhandled you?"

"Not so far," Cora said.

"Too bad. I'm adding up the charges here. A few more, and I'll be able to take a nice vacation."

"Are the handcuffs necessary, Perkins?" Crowley said.

Perkins shrugged. "The young lady didn't wish to accompany me. I didn't wish to have my eyes scratched out."

"Ah," Becky said. "May I add resisting arrest to the list of false charges for which I'll be seeking compensation?"

"I think we can dispense with the handcuffs, Perkins."

Becky's wrists were handcuffed behind her back. Perkins bent down, fitted the key.

"Nice back there, isn't it?" Cora said. She was gratified to see the young officer blush.

"Ah, Miss Baldwin, is it?" Crowley said.

"Yes."

"Are you appearing for Miss Felton?"

"I'm appearing because I was dragged here in handcuffs."

Sergeant Crowley exhaled slowly through his mouth. He seemed to be trying awfully hard to control his temper. "I was not so much concerned with how you got here as the capacity in which you appear."

"I appear in the capacity of a woman who's been wrongfully arrested on a bogus charge."

The sergeant waved it away. "Yeah, yeah. I got that. I'm asking Cora Felton here some questions. She is at the very least a witness in a homicide. We assume she'd like to do her civic duty and assist in an investigation. We're sure she has no wish to obstruct the investigation."

"Was that a threat or a bluff?"

"He doesn't bluff," Cora said.

"That's a threat? Excellent. The list of charges grows."

"Yeah, yeah, yeah. You're clever with words. You passed the bar and all that. I need your client's help in clearing up this crime. She refused to talk until her attorney was present. We have followed the letter of the law in producing her attorney. Now, you want to have a pissing contest or you want to get on with it?"

"Crude, isn't he?" Cora said.

Becky shrugged. "Frankly, I prefer it to patronizing and wolfish. Look, Detective—"

"I'm a sergeant."

"Be still my heart. Look, Sergeant. We got theater tickets. Is there anything that's going to satisfy you short of a full confession?"

"That's practically what she said."

"And you wouldn't let her confess without me. Kudos. I'm proud of you, Sergeant."

"If you want to get out of here, let your client clean up some minor details for me."

"Such as?"

"He wants to know what I was doing in that apartment with a recently fired gun."

Becky nodded. "And what would you consider a *major* detail, Sergeant?"

"You see my problem," Crowley said. "Without an explanation, it's hard to imagine letting her go."

"And with an explanation, you'll thank her and give her a ride Uptown?"

Crowley exhaled again. "You want to keep sparring, that's your business. I'm not the one pressed for time."

"Good point. Let me help you out here, Sergeant. What's the name of the dead man?"

Crowley shook his head. "You're the one providing the information."

Becky grimaced. "That's going to be less than helpful if we don't know what we're talking about. You want to know our relationship with the dead man. Assuming we never met the man in question, it's impossible to know if we've ever had any dealings with him unless we know who he is."

"Does that mean you've had dealings with him?"

"I have no idea. Who is he?"

Sergeant Crowley frowned.

Cora grinned. She understood his frustration. He really wanted an answer, but Becky's logic was hard to ignore.

"The dead man would appear to be the occupant of the apartment. In support of that contention is the fact that he appeared to live there, that he was identified by the doorman, that he had in his pocket a wallet with identification for the gentleman in question, including photo IDs that certainly seemed to look like the dead man, with the exception of being alive. I'm still waiting on fingerprinting, DNA testing, and the identification of a close relative, but I do not think that it would be misleading for me to suggest to you that the dead man was Charles Kessington."

"Couldn't have split those hairs better myself, Sergeant," Becky said. "In light of that startling revelation, I think we are prepared to help you out. Providing we don't compromise my client's rights while we do so. So, assuming the hypothesis that my client and I might have had some dealings with the decedent, let's see what we can do."

"I don't want to assume a hypothesis."

"Well, unless you want to get an ADA down here so I can say charge her or release her, that's what you're going to get. The problem is once I say charge her or release her, the information's going to dry up rather quickly."

"Is that a threat?"

"No," Becky said. "It's a bluff. Call it and see what you get."

"I like her," Cora said. "Don't you like her?"

Sergeant Crowley glowered. "Hit me with your hypothetical."

"Fine," Becky said. "For the sake of argument, say the decedent called me up and asked to retain my services as an attorney. Say he didn't want to see me in my office and didn't want me to come to his. Say I was reluctant to go alone to the gentleman's penthouse apartment, and therefore hired Ms. Felton, who had done some investigation for me in the past, to come along as an armed chaperone/bodyguard."

"What about the gun?"

Becky smiled, gestured to Cora. "My client hawks breakfast cereal to schoolchildren. Would you really expect her to wrestle a would-be rapist into submission?"

"I wouldn't expect her to shoot him in the head."

"Neither would I. I would consider that exceeding her authority."

"Oh, for Christ's sake. She was holding the gun. Are you claiming she found it and picked it up? That is beyond stupid, even for the rankest amateur detective."

"Thank you for not suspecting me of doing that, Sergeant," Cora said.

"I'm waiting for an explanation."

"The killer had the gun. She surprised him in the bedroom rifling the safe. When he aimed the murder weapon at her, she fired back."

"You didn't say hypothetically."

"Doesn't matter. There is a huge hypothetical parenthesis around this entire conversation."

"You are now claiming the discharged weapon found in your client's possession is her own gun?"

"You didn't say hypothetical either."

"I thought we had a big parenthesis. Or does that just work for you?"

"I am saying the gun found in my client's possession had absolutely nothing to do with the murder. Compare a bullet fired from it with the fatal bullet, and that will be abundantly clear. If you step on it, we might even make the curtain."

"Hypothetically."

"No, it's a real curtain."

"You claim your client fired this gun in the bedroom?"

"What's wrong with that?"

"There was no bullet found."

"The bullet went out the hypothetical window," Cora said. "Surely you have a ballistics expert familiar enough with firearms to be able to discharge a weapon."

The sergeant snatched up the phone, punched in a number. "Denton, Crowley. Who's got the Charles Kessington evidence? . . . Yeah I'll hold on." He cupped the phone, said, "Ordinarily there's a chain of evidence, but when there's something as important as theater tickets . . . Un-huh. Thanks. Can you transfer me? . . . Yeah, it does that to me, too." He pushed a button on the phone, got a dial tone, punched another number in. "Sergeant Crowley. Redburn there? . . . Hi, Sam. Look. You're doing the Kessington case? We got a gun recovered at the scene, shot fired. . . . Yeah, that one. You match it up with the fatal bullet yet? . . . Yeah, I know it just happened. . . . Any way to hurry it along? . . . Who? . . . Millhouse?" The sergeant grimaced. "No, I understand."

He hung up the phone. "Bad news. The postmortem's in the hands of an ME who positively hates the theater."

"You're kidding," Cora said.

"Yes, I am. He's just notoriously slow. The result is the same. The guy's a human rain delay. Calls from impatient ballistics experts just piss him off. Nothing to do but wait."

"Oh, for Christ's sake."

"The guy knows we need it. He'll call as soon as it comes in. In the meantime, what did the decedent want to consult you about?"

"I don't know," Becky said.

"Hypothetically?"

"No, I really don't know. I have never at any point in time been told what this guy wanted to consult me about. By him, or by anybody else. If you give any credence to my hypothetical at all, you may take it for granted that the man approached me about a matter which he did not in any way explain."

"If you didn't recognize him, this would not have been a face-to-face meeting."

"No, it would have been a phone call."

"Where to?"

"To my office. In Bakerhaven, Connecticut."

"Where was he calling from?"

"You ever get a phone call, Sergeant? I don't know about you, but I have no way of knowing where they're from."

"Some people have caller ID."

"And some private calls are blocked."

"Are you saying that was the case?"

"I'm saying I don't know where the call came from. You can draw your own conclusions. You can also make your own investigation. I would assume these weren't local calls. Perhaps the telephone company could be of some assistance."

"You also might want to put out a dragnet for an armed man dressed in black with a stocking over his head," Cora said. "Though by now a really clever murderer might have removed the stocking."

Sergeant Crowley ignored her, said to Becky, "Is that all you care to tell us?"

"That is hypothetically all we know."

"Actually," Crowley said, "there was one other thing."

"Oh? What's that?"

"The crossword puzzle."

Cora Felton uttered a remark more suitable to a biker bar.

"Easy, Cora."

"No, I'm interested in that reaction. Your client appears to have some opinion about the crossword puzzle. Would you care to elaborate?"

"No, I would not care to elaborate," Cora said. "There's a dead man. He had a crossword on him. I don't know why. I don't know how it got there. It's got nothing to do with me."

"You're the Puzzle Lady."

"That doesn't mean I'm responsible for every crossword created since the dawn of time."

"No. But it happens to be your field of expertise. Don't you think that's significant?"

"I certainly do. It's significant because morons who don't know any better will assume it has something to do with me."

"Now, now, now, now, now," Becky said. "What my client meant to say is that since she knows absolutely nothing about the crossword puzzle, it is either a monstrous coincidence, or else someone has deliberately gone out of their way to make it appear she knows something about it."

"Interesting," Sergeant Crowley said. "And who knew she was going to be calling on the decedent?"

"See?" Becky said. "This is why the whole question of the crossword puzzle is so unfair. You are now asking me to speculate on who might have known of a hypothetical happenstance."

"Hypothetical happenstance," Cora said. "I like that. That could be a Perry Mason title. *The Case of the Hypothetical Happenstance.*"

"I'm not amused. There's a puzzle. You're the Puzzle Lady. You want to tell me what it means?"

"I have no idea what it means."

"I mean you want to solve it?"

"No."

"I'm not asking you to reveal anything. I'm just asking you to solve the puzzle."

"Which I have no intention of doing. It's a crossword puzzle. It doesn't look that hard. I'm sure if your detectives all put their heads together, they ought to be able to figure it out."

"I'd like your opinion."

Before Cora could give him her opinion, Becky jumped in. "I think we have a gray area here, Sergeant. If you would like to hire Cora Felton as a police consultant, I'm sure that could be arranged. You would first have to release her from custody and dismiss any possible charges."

"Oh, now you're my agent?" Cora said. "Look. I don't want to be hired as a police consultant. I'm just not willing to concede that anything involving a crossword concerns me. But I don't want to be unreasonable. When you get this solved, Sergeant, I'll be happy to look it over and tell you what I think. I can tell you right now, I won't think much."

"That should do it," Becky said. "So, since your own department can't work fast enough to get the ballistics evidence that would clear her, why don't you ring the ADA and see if he could expedite an arraignment so we can post bail and get out of here and go to the theater. After all, I'd hate to ruin a trip to New York over just one dead body."

Sergeant Crowley said nothing. He stared at Becky for some time, considering. Cora wasn't sure what he was going to do, but the phrase *throw the book at her* came to mind. She wondered what charges the man could think up. Obstruction of justice seemed likely. It was also less harsh than *accessory to murder.* Or simply *murder.*

Crowley snatched up the phone. "Phillips. Bring me a couple of Form Triple-E." He plunked the phone down again.

They sat in silence.

A young man in a white shirt and tie came in, handed the sergeant some forms, and went out.

Crowley handed one each to Cora and Becky.

Cora looked up from the form. "Hey. This isn't Form Triple-E."

"That's a euphemism. They're waiver forms."

"Waiver?"

"Waiver of false arrest. Any time we have a lawyer in here screaming false arrest, the ADAs like us to have 'em sign 'em."

"We're not signing any waivers of false arrest," Becky said.

Crowley nodded, as if that was exactly what he expected. "That's too bad. You'll have to go back to the holding cells while I schedule an arraignment. I have certain discretionary powers, but I can't let suspects go when they're threatening me with false arrest."

"Let suspects go?" Cora said.

"The ADA would chew my ass. Letting you go is tantamount to admitting you shouldn't have been picked up in the first place. At least with a lawyer involved."

"You're letting us go?" Cora said.

Crowley shrugged. "It's not like you're a flight risk. Everyone in America knows your face. I can't imagine your attorney would be screaming for a ballistics test if she thought it would prove you're guilty. I'd just as soon dismiss the charges, as long as it doesn't get me in trouble. So if you'd like to voluntarily take a paraffin test, since your attorney has only hypothetically conceded you fired a gun, and if you're willing to sign waivers saying you won't sue me for doing so . . ."

Crowley shrugged again. "I'd just as soon let you go."

"So how'd you like the play?" Cora said as they drove the Hutchinson River Parkway into the Merritt.

"Frankly," Becky said, "it wasn't uppermost in my mind."

"Okay. Aside from that, Mrs. Lincoln, how did you like the play?"

"It was wonderful. Under any other circumstances, I'd have had a really good time. As it was, I sat there obsessing on the last thing that damn sergeant said."

"The fact he let us go?"

"No. The crossword puzzle."

Cora reacted well to the comment by not driving off the road. "Must we come back to the crossword puzzle?"

"Yeah, we must," Becky said. "It's the most intriguing thing about the murder. I wish we had a copy."

"Why didn't you ask for one?"

"I was afraid to. After insisting it didn't mean anything."

"He knew we were lying."

"How would he know that?"

"It *has* to mean something. Everywhere I go, there's a goddamned crossword puzzle. It always means something."

"You always insist it doesn't."

"That's so I won't have to solve them. The fact it's there is significant. And you know what's really significant?"

"What?"

"Who knew I was coming? The guy hired *you*. He didn't hire *me*. He didn't *ask* you to bring me. By all rights, he didn't *want* you to bring me. He didn't know I was coming."

"I'll buy that."

"But the killer knew I was coming? How does that make any sense?"

"It doesn't," Becky said. "Which is why I didn't want to show too much interest in the crossword puzzle. And make it look as if I thought it *was* significant."

"It *is* significant."

"You're going around again, Cora."

"And then the guy lets us go. What, is he nuts? If I had to make a list of the courses of action available to the sergeant, letting us go would not have been in the top ten. Hell, I doubt if it would have made the list."

"His reasons made sense."

"You find that reassuring? I don't. He's just a dumb cop. You expect his reasons to make sense? I wouldn't expect him to reason beyond 'she had the gun, she's guilty.' "

"Maybe he was acting on instructions," Becky said.

"Who from?"

"The ADA."

"There wasn't an ADA present. Most of what he was acting on was what we gave him in the interview."

"We didn't give him anything."

"Exactly," Cora said. "You think an ADA lets us walk without telling a story."

"Maybe he's just a nice guy."

Cora offered a brief, pungent ejaculation.

"Even if he's not a nice guy, I'm not sure he deserved that," Becky said.

Cora didn't answer. She kept her eyes on the road ahead and said casually, "Becky."

"What?"

"Don't look around, but there's a black sedan following us."

Becky blinked, managed to restrain herself from looking. "How do you know it's following us?"

"It's been behind us since the city."

"A lot of cars have been behind us since the city. If you drive from New York to Connecticut, this is sort of the way you go."

"Laugh it off if you want to. I'll be a lot happier if he doesn't take 7 North."

"If he's going north, he'll take 7 North or 8 North. Seven North is first, it's shorter, it's more likely, we take it. You gonna freak out if he does?"

"Oh, for Christ's sake." Cora switched on the right-hand blinker.

"What are you doing?"

"Stopping for gas."

"You filled up on the way down."

"Okay, you need to go to the bathroom."

"No, I don't."

"All right, *I* need to go to the bathroom. You stay here and spot the tail."

Cora pulled into one of the many service stations that line the Merritt Parkway. She drove by the pumps and parked in a head-in diagonal space.

"You'll have to switch seats, though. It's easier to watch the rearview mirror from the driver's side."

"Is this just a ploy to get me to drive again?" Becky said.

"God, I hope so."

Cora got out of the car and headed back toward the station.

The black sedan hadn't followed them past the pumps, but on the far side of the station, a car was idling in the shadows. With the headlights shining at her, she couldn't tell if it was the same vehicle.

Cora had an instant decision to make. Should she stride up to the car, bang on the window, and demand to know what the driver was doing? Or should she pretend she hadn't spotted him and see what he did. Her instinct was to promote the confrontation—Cora always favored action over inaction—but approaching a car head-on in the dark was a risky proposition. Even cops used caution. Those who didn't occasionally got their heads blown off. The killer had a gun. He wasn't afraid to use it. He might not take kindly to having been spotted.

Cora reached the front door of the station. The driver's face still wasn't visible. Damn. In detective novels, she'd see his face in the glow of the cigarette. No one smoked anymore.

Still grumbling to herself, Cora went inside. She had a faint hope that maybe the guy'd follow her in and Becky would see him.

Becky couldn't see a thing. She'd moved to the driver's seat and the mirror was angled just fine, but she couldn't see around the station. A car on the other side wouldn't be visible unless it pulled up to the pumps.

Becky watched Cora go into the station. No one followed her in. No car pulled up to the pumps. Had any car driven past while they were arguing? No, it had not. And here she was, sitting in the parking lot like a fool, where she couldn't see a damn thing.

It occurred to Becky she could use a stick of gum. She didn't have to chew it, she just had to buy it. For less than a buck, she could pop in and out of the station and get a look at the other side.

As she drew near the pumps, she could see a car parked in the shadows on the far side of the station. The motor wasn't running, and the headlights were off. Becky couldn't see if there was anyone in the driver's seat.

But Becky's attention wasn't focused on the car. She was too distracted by the man with his coat collar pulled up and his hat down over his face who had just passed the corner of the pumps and was headed up the steps into the store.

Whoops.

Was the man from the car? Was that the same car? Was the man following Cora into the service station to make sure she didn't slip out some side door?

Did the man know who Becky was? Had he recognized her as the other woman in the car he was following?

Becky bit her lip. If he did know who she was, stopping and turning around would be a dead giveaway. The advantage she and Cora had was that the man didn't know they'd spotted him. If she blew it, Cora would be furious. Of course, having been arrested for murder, Cora was in a mood to be furious. She'd probably be mad at her just for getting out of the car.

Becky barely broke stride. She skipped up the steps and came in the door of the service station right on the man's heels.

The man glanced around. So did Becky. Cora wasn't there. The man headed in the direction of the rest rooms. If he was headed for the men's room, Becky should snag Cora out of the ladies' and they should drive off and leave him stranded.

He wasn't. He stopped just before the door to the women's room and began inspecting one of the stand-up coolers of soda.

Becky headed in the opposite direction and looked for gum. There was none. Damn it. There was no one in line at the counter; she could just buy it and go.

Becky strode up to the clerk. She worked behind a glass window, practically unnecessary these days, with everyone using credit cards and nobody paying cash.

"You got any gum?" Becky said. She felt like a fool. The woman was chewing gum.

The woman pointed down.

Becky looked. There was a box of Trident on the bottom shelf. She grabbed a pack, slid it through the window.

The woman scanned it. They scanned everything these days. It was a dollar one with tax. Becky didn't have a penny. She slid two dollars through the window.

The woman pushed one back, said, "Close enough."

Becky grabbed the gum and turned around.

The man with the hat over his eyes was still hanging out by the women's room, pretending to look at soda. Becky ignored the man, went out the front door.

The car was still parked in the shadows. Becky wasn't surprised. It occurred to her the guy would have to sprint for it when Cora came out of the women's room. She wondered how he'd do that if she was watching. It was an intriguing thought. If the guy didn't know he'd been spotted, he wouldn't want to be. His dilemma would be the best of all possible worlds.

Becky stopped on the steps, unwrapped the pack of gum. No need to rush. Let's see, these packs had drawstrings, didn't they? Where was it? On the end. No, the other end.

Her fingernails were long enough to pry it up just fine, but too long to grip it well. How could she pull it around the pack?

Hmm. Not that big a problem. How long could she pretend to be thwarted by it? Not that the man would see her do it; he'd just come out and find her unwrapping a stick of gum. Would it occur to him, *Boy that took a long time, how klutzy is this broad?* It might if he was following her; otherwise, why would he even notice?

Becky had the top of the pack open. She wrestled a stick of gum out. Okay, no way unwrapping a stick is as tough as unwrapping a pack.

Becky heard footsteps behind her. Without looking around, she couldn't tell if it was him or if it was someone else. She unwrapped the gum, fed it into her mouth. As she did, the man with the hat over his face came down the steps. He took no notice of her, headed back in the direction of his car.

When he reached the end of the pumps, he hung a right and

walked around the back of the Mini Cooper parked there. He had a bottle of soda in his hand. He hopped into the Mini Cooper, started the engine, and took off.

Becky felt foolish as hell. She turned and walked back to Cora's Toyota and slipped into the driver's seat.

Moments later, the door opened and Cora slid into the passenger seat.

"Had to go to the bathroom after all," Cora said. "So. Any luck? You see the guy?"

Becky was grateful for the question. It was one she could answer truthfully without having to embellish. "No," she said.

"I didn't think so. There's a car parked in the shadows the other side of the station. Pull out, see if he follows."

"Fine," Becky said. She started the engine.

Cora looked at Becky, frowned. "Are you chewing gum?"

The black sedan followed them up the Merritt Parkway and turned north on Route 7 when they did.

"Believe me now?" Cora said.

"I believed you then," Becky said. "I just didn't want to."

"Well, it answers one question."

"What's that?"

"Why Crowley let us go."

"You mean that's him?"

"Well, not him personally. But one of his boys. Perkins, perhaps. He seemed to like you."

"You really think it's the cops?"

"I prefer it to the killer."

"Cora."

"What do you want me to say? 'There, there, Becky, it's all right. The killer isn't on your tail.' I have no idea who's in the car behind us. But I prefer knowing about it to *not* knowing about it. Anyway, whoever it is, it's interesting."

"Unless it's a businessman on his way home," Becky said.

"Who followed us to a service station on the Merritt, parked in the shadows while we went inside, and then followed us out of the station?"

"All right, a rather weird businessman on his way home."

"Hey, I'll give the guy the benefit of the doubt if he'll just turn off."

He didn't. The black sedan was behind them all the way up Route 7, turned off when they did, followed from a discreet distance over the local roads. By the time Becky took the last turn toward Bakerhaven, there was no doubt about it.

"Okay, Nancy Drew, you're up," Cora said.

"Huh?" Becky said.

"Where's your car parked?"

"Front of the library."

"Excellent," Cora said. "Hop out, get in your car, and drive to the mall."

"I live right down the alley."

"Yeah, but you don't want to go there. Head for the mall. If the guy follows you, I'll drive up on his tail and get his plate number."

"What do I do then?"

"Well, since the mall's closed, I wouldn't hang out there. Circle the parking lot and drive home."

Cora pulled up across from the library.

"I won't be able to sleep knowing someone's watching me," Becky said.

"Don't worry. I'll sneak up on the guy and blow his head off."

"Cora."

"You don't like that idea? Okay, call the cops. Dan Finley will make a point of cruising by. He's as smitten as that Perkins guy. You know, it would be funny if Finley was protecting you from Perkins."

"Yeah, a laugh riot."

"But I don't think it'll happen. I think he'll follow me."

"Why?"

"Because of the crossword puzzle. If it weren't for the crossword puzzle, I'd say he was after you. But you start throwing puzzles in the mix, someone's out to get me."

"You're probably right. So if he follows you, I tag along and get his plate number?"

"Yeah. Not so close he kills you, just close enough to read the plate."

"And if he turns around and comes after me?"

"I've got a gun."

"No, you *don't*. The police kept it to compare the bullet."

"So don't let him catch you."

"Cora."

"Relax. He'll never know you're there."

"What do you want me to do when I get the plate number?"

"Go home and call me. I need to know someone's sitting on the house anyway."

"But—"

"Get out of the car already. Fella's going to think we're lovers."

Becky gave Cora a look and got out.

Cora got out of the passenger seat, walked around to the driver's side. "See you tomorrow," Cora said. She hopped in and took off.

Cora glanced in the rearview mirror. The guy was still following her. As expected. Despite what she told Becky, Cora felt a slight rush of adrenaline. She didn't speed up or slow down, just kept going. She drove home without incident and turned up the driveway. The guy had followed all the way. Cora couldn't see Becky, but she knew she was back there.

Cora parked the car in the drive and walked across the lawn. The lights were out in the upstairs addition. It was after midnight. Cora had left the light on in the living room. She was happy to have it.

The living room drapes were drawn. Cora pushed the curtain

aside a crack and peered out. Nothing was moving, everything was quiet, there were no lights down by the road. Not that it meant anything. If the guy was watching the house, he'd have killed his lights. There was no way to know.

Assuming it was the guy. Assuming it wasn't some stupid cop.

The phone rang and Cora jumped a mile. Good God, she was wound up! Who the hell could it be at this hour? For one time Cora wished she had a phone in the living room. She had to go in the office or the kitchen to answer, and she didn't want to leave the window.

The phone rang again. Cora took one last look and sprinted for the kitchen.

She snatched the receiver off the wall. "Hello!" she snarled.

"Well, I like that. Last time I do you a favor."

Cora blinked. "Becky? How'd you get home so fast?"

"I have a cell phone, Cora."

"Oh. Right."

"Boy are you nervous. Relax. The guy went right on by your driveway and kept going."

"You're kidding."

"No. Maybe he *is* just some guy on the way home. I mean, someone's gotta live around here, right?"

"You sure he didn't turn around and double back?"

"I sure am. I'm still following him."

"You're driving with a cell phone?"

"Don't worry. If I get picked up, I know a good lawyer."

"Becky. It's not funny. If this guy sees you—"

"He won't. When I passed your house, I dropped back. He's way up ahead."

"Did you get the license number?"

"Of course I got the license number. You want it?"

"You gonna read the number on the cell phone driving a car?"

"Why not? I wrote it driving a car. Here we go. It's two, seven—"

"I don't have a pencil. Hang on."

The phone had a long cord. Cora crossed to the sink, wrenched open the counter door to the left. It was a miscellaneous drawer, with everything from rubber bands to razor blades to plastic spoons to screws and bolts and bottle-stoppers. Cora scrabbled through.

"Just a minute. I think there's one in this drawer."

"Take your time. It's a nice night for a drive."

"Got it!" Cora snatched up the pencil. "Oh, hell!"

"What?"

"The point's broken. Hang on."

"Just let me know when you're ready."

Cora dug her fingernails in to break the wood off the lead. "There we go. Lay it on me."

"It's two, seven, nine— Oh, hell! He's coming back!"

And the phone went dead.

Chapter 12

Cora had a moment of dread. Oh God, he got her!

Thoughts flashed through her brain like lightning, laying on layer upon layer of guilt and dread. *Becky's dead! It's my fault! It's not my fault! Schmuck, what difference does that make? She didn't tell me the license number, now I'll never know. Schmuck, how can you think that? I'm going to kill him! Yeah, like that'll help Becky. Idiot, who cares?*

Cora snatched her purse off the table, raced to the front door, flung it open. Realized she didn't have her gun. She cursed, ran to the bedroom, wrenched open her bottom dresser drawer, and pawed through the clothes she never wore for the spare gun her ex-husband Melvin had given her. She found it, jerked it out, flipped it open. It was loaded. She flipped it closed and ran out the door.

In the car, she wasted moments fishing for her keys. She gunned the motor without regard for whether it woke Sherry, Aaron, and the baby, rocketed down the driveway, and hung a left.

How far was it? Becky said the guy turned around and doubled back. But she'd been on the phone a long time before that. And she hadn't called before she passed the drive. So how far could that be? No farther than she could drive in that amount of time. But what amount of time? How long was it?

Cora sped down the country road, her high beams lighting up the woods and fields and an occasional house along the way. No place a car could have turned off. No car off the road. Where were they?

She reached Jackson Corners, so named though it boasted no landmarks of any sort, no houses, nor any corners. Except for the lone street sign, you wouldn't know where you were. The only excuse for calling it Jackson Corners was that Jackson Road went two directions. Which way had they gone? Had they turned at all? If they'd turned, Becky would have commented on it. Yeah, if they turned off before the black sedan turned around. So they must have gone past. There was no way they could be on Jackson Road. Unless Becky had taken one of the side roads to get away from him after he turned around.

Assuming she got away.

Cora flew by Jackson Corners and kept going.

A car coming around the bend nearly hit her head-on. Not that the car was going fast or that it was on the wrong side of the road. But Cora was. She cut the corner, and suddenly there it was, bright headlights and a blaring horn and sickening squeal of brakes. Cora wrenched the steering wheel to the right, careened across the road. She almost cleared it but not quite. She could hear the ding of her rear bumper catching the driver's side front bumper of the oncoming car. She fishtailed, spun the wheel, and 180ed. Her car skidded backwards across the road and stopped with a bone-jarring thump against something hard that snapped her head like a whip.

Cora straightened in her seat and looked over the dashboard just in time to see the headlights of a car bearing down on her. She instinctively flung up her hands as if they could protect her from a couple of tons of onrushing steel.

A car pulled to a stop in front of her. An ashen-faced man got out, ran over, and wrenched the door open.

"Good God, are you all right?"

"Who are you?" Cora said stupidly.

"I couldn't avoid you. I nicked your bumper. I saw you fishtail."

"Uh-huh," Cora said. She unsnapped her seat belt.

"You probably shouldn't move."

Cora heaved herself out of the car, pushed by him to look at his.

"My car's fine. I didn't skid."

Cora ignored him, walked around so his headlights weren't blinding her.

His car was a blue Subaru.

She turned back to the driver. "Where you coming from?"

"Over the mountain."

"You pass anyone?"

"No."

"I mean going my direction."

"No. No one."

"Any car off the road?"

"Just yours."

"Comedian," Cora muttered.

"Huh?"

"I gotta go."

The man was amazingly polite, considering Cora had nearly killed him. He was also a middle-age stick-in-the-mud fuddy duddy who insisted on exchanging insurance information. Cora nearly had to pull the gun on him to escape from his clutches. She fled the scene of the accident, and spent a half hour searching the side roads for any sign of Becky's car.

It was long gone.

Chapter

1 3

Cora came in the front door to find Sherry and Becky sipping coffee in the living room.

"What are you doing here?" Cora demanded.

"I live here," Sherry said.

"Not you, damn it."

"You don't have a cell phone," Becky said.

"Huh?"

"If you had a cell phone, I could have called you and told you where I was. But, oh no, I call here, get no answer, don't know where you are."

"I was looking for you."

"I knew that. I just didn't know where."

"So you came here and woke up Sherry."

"I was awake. Someone started a jet plane in the driveway."

"It wasn't me," Becky said. "I was quiet as a mouse."

"She let herself in," Sherry said. "I looked out the window to see if it was you, saw her car in the drive."

"Oh, for Christ's sake." Cora slumped down on the couch.

"Have some coffee. It'll calm you down."

"Coffee?"

"Decaffeinated. Hot and comforting. Like hot cocoa. Without all the calories."

"I thought he got you."

"Got me?"

"I thought he realized he had a tail and came back to rub you out."

"I'm fine. Sherry was just filling me in on the joys of motherhood."

"Jennifer's got a strep throat. She's not happy about it. Sounds like an angry buzz saw cutting metal."

"She likes telling me stuff like that," Becky said. "Thinks it makes up for stealing my man."

"Don't you think stealing's a little harsh," Sherry said, "after several years' absence?"

"Hey, when I brand 'em, it's for life."

"Damn it," Cora said. "I've been frightened out of my wits and nearly wrecked the car. You wanna tell me what the hell happened?"

"Wrecked the car?" Sherry said.

"Nearly, nearly. I banged the bumper."

"On what?"

"Well, technically, the other guy banged the bumper. I slid off the road."

"What!"

Cora described the accident.

"Idiot," Sherry said. "You could have been killed."

"But I wasn't. I thought *she* was."

"I just dropped my cell phone," Becky said.

"What?"

"He startled me. Turning around like that. Suddenly there's bright lights coming at me. I dropped my cell phone."

"He wasn't after you?"

"Hell, no. Went by me like a house on fire. Took off down the road. I swung a U-turn, tried to keep up. I think he turned left on Mountain Road."

"You think?"

"There were lights in that direction, none up ahead. I tried to follow, but it's twisty, there's a zillion forks, he could have gone the other way on any one of them. When I came out on Colson and didn't see him, I figured he was gone."

"You went all the way to Colson Road?"

"Not that far if you're doing ninety."

"You went ninety on Mountain Road? And I'm the one who had the accident. Damn it, why didn't you call me back?"

"The phone was under the seat. I figured you'd be pissed if I was driving Mountain Road at ninety miles an hour while groping under the seat."

"But you got the license number?"

Becky smiled. "See, Sherry? She wasn't worried about me. She was afraid she wouldn't get her license number."

"Yeah," Sherry said. She put her cup down on the coffee table, cocked her head at Cora. "So, you wanna address the elephant in the room?"

"Why, Sherry Carter! Becky may be your rival, but don't you think that's a little harsh?"

"That's feeble, even for you, Cora." Sherry shook her head pityingly. "You must be really worried."

"Wrong elephant?"

"You got arrested for murder."

"Oh. That pachyderm."

"Were you going to get to that?"

"I figured by now you and Becky had hashed it over and planned my defense."

"From what Becky tells me, your defense is pretty straightforward. The police compare a bullet from your gun to the bullet in the body and have to concede you didn't fire the fatal shot."

"For this I pay you a huge retainer," Cora told Becky.

"Glad you brought it up," Becky said.

"I shouldn't pay you anything. You let the guy get away."

"I got the plate. Of course, it may not mean anything."

"How can it not mean something? What was the guy doing if he wasn't following us?"

"He was on his way home."

"So when he sees a car behind him, he naturally pulls a one-eighty and proceeds to ditch you."

"It's late, he was tired, he missed his turn. When he realized it, he tried to make up the time."

"You really believe that?"

Becky shrugged. "I'm a lawyer. I just have to create reasonable doubt."

"It's not funny, Becky. I thought he might have got you."

"An insurance salesman from Bakerhaven?"

"If that's what he is," Cora said.

But she didn't believe it.

Chapter

14

Cora walked into the police station and dropped a piece of paper on Officer Dan Finley's desk. "Got time to run a license plate?"

"Will it get me into trouble?"

"When have I ever got you into trouble?"

"All the time. You hold out on me and I'm in trouble for not getting you to talk. You talk, and I'm in trouble for listening."

"Gee, Dan. What brought this on?"

"Chief wants to see you."

"Oh?"

"I've been trying to call you all morning."

"I wasn't home."

"I figured that when you didn't answer your phone and Sherry answered hers and said you weren't there."

"You bothered Sherry?"

"The chief really wants to talk to you. He can't, and he's blaming me."

"Ducking phone calls."

"Cora."

"I've been driving around trying to think. Which isn't easy. You try getting arrested for murder."

"I wouldn't do that."

"Do I have to instruct you again? Anyone can be arrested. It is no indication that they have committed a crime."

Harper exhaled, shook his head. "I'm too tired to spar. Would you mind telling me what's going on?"

"Do I need my lawyer present?"

"What in the world for?"

"I don't know. Were you planning on blabbing to the New York cops? Call that sergeant back, get a few brownie points?"

"Hadn't crossed my mind." Harper shrugged. "Has now."

"Come on, Chief. Let's not posture. I'll say the word 'hypothetical' and we'll talk off the record."

"Is it that bad?"

"No, that's the whole point. It's not bad at all. But with other cops involved, things can get a little sticky." Cora fished her cigarettes out of her purse. "Solve your break-in?"

"You can't smoke in here."

"You want me to ignore my lawyer's advice, bad-mouth the New York cops, and solve your illegal entry for you, you can damn well let me smoke." Before the chief could protest, she fired one up. "It's lit, Chief. Throw me out if you want."

"You gonna tell me what happened?"

"I'll tell you what *might* have happened. And if it goes any further, I'll deny it."

"Cora."

"Relax, Chief. It's not that bad."

Cora gave Chief Harper an expurgated version of what had happened. She left out the bit about playing chicken at midnight out past Jackson Corners. Even without that episode, there was a lot to tell.

"It's a wonder you're not in jail," Harper said.

"Well, now you're the golden boy. You found me. Pick up the phone, tell him I'm on my way in."

Dan picked up the receiver.

"While I'm talking to him, you can trace that plate."

"Cora."

"Too busy?" Cora picked up the number, turned toward the front door. "I can come back later."

Dan snatched the paper out of her hand.

Cora went into the office. Chief Harper was on the phone. "She's here now," he said, and slammed it down.

"Finley?"

Harper gave her a look.

"The kid's persistent. Tracked me like a bloodhound."

"Damn it, Cora, where have you been?"

"Why do I think you know?"

"I got a call from the NYPD. A Sergeant Crowley, I believe it is. Wanted to know if I have any control over the good citizens of Bakerhaven. Seems one of them drove to New York yesterday and shot someone."

"I don't know how these rumors get started."

"Were you or were you not arrested for murder yesterday?"

"You say that as if it were a bad thing. It's no crime to be arrested. You're innocent until proven guilty."

"I'm not interested in the technical merits of the case. Did you or not shoot a man?"

"Would I do something like that?"

"Yes. Repeatedly."

"But I wouldn't kill anyone."

"I beg to differ. Would you like me to refresh your memory?"

"I never shot anyone in cold blood. That's what we're talking about here. A cold-blooded, premeditated crime. As my lawyer will have no problem demonstrating."

"Where have you been all morning?"

"I wondered about that myself. I figured the NYPD called you and you put in a good word."

Harper shook his head. "First I heard about it was this morning. And the word I put in was not good."

On the way out, Dan Finley handed Cora Felton a folded piece of paper.

"What's this?"

"Your plate number. Maybe you can do something with it. I couldn't."

"What?"

"Plate's not registered."

"What the hell does that mean?"

"It's an unregistered number. No one has it."

"Someone does."

"If you say so. Any chance you got the number wrong?"

"Absolutely not," Cora said, but she wondered how well Becky could have written it while driving with one hand.

"Anyway, I can't help you with the plate. As far as the registry of motor vehicles is concerned, it doesn't exist."

"Who would have an unregistered plate?"

"No one."

"How about an undercover cop?"

Dan shook his head.

"Why not?"

"An undercover cop would have an *untraceable* plate."

"What's the difference?"

"An untraceable plate is registered to a person who doesn't exist. Or to an address that doesn't exist. Or to a car that doesn't exist. It's registered, it's just registered wrong. Anyone tracing the plate won't find anything suspicious. It would have layers and layers of insulation. It would take a real investigation just to find out the plate was bogus."

Dan was enjoying showing off. "An unregistered plate, you try to trace it, it isn't registered at all, you know right away it's phony."

"Where'd you learn that?" Cora said.

Dan flushed. "Actually, it was on this cop show."

"Right."

"But you get the point. As soon as the plate doesn't exist, you know it couldn't be some little old lady from the local bridge club."

"I play bridge," Cora said.

Dan's mouth fell open. "Not that young women don't play bridge. Or men," he added lamely.

Cora went out, sat in her car, and thought that over. Things were adding up, and she didn't like what they were adding up to. She and Becky had been followed home by a car with an unregistered plate. Whatever the reason, it was scary as hell. Someone had gone to a lot of trouble to make sure he wasn't identified. Or she, Cora thought, echoing Dan Finley's PC nod to sexism, though she didn't really think the driver was a woman. The killer was a man.

At least she was pretty sure he was a man. All she really saw was a figure dressed entirely in black who had his back to her, and who had sprinted away with a stocking over his face.

And a gun in his hand. That was fairly distracting. Kept her from noticing any anatomical clues as to the weapon-wielder's gender.

But was the driver the killer? Or was he, despite what Dan might have seen on TV, an undercover officer keeping tabs on the suspects?

Either way, Cora didn't like it.

"Are you following me?"

Sergeant Crowley cocked his head at Cora. "I beg your pardon?"

"It's a simple enough question, Sergeant, even for a police officer. But let me break it down for you. Are you having me tailed? Have you authorized surveillance? Are detectives from your department, or any other department, or any other policemen that you know of, following me around to see what I do?"

"Wow," Crowley said.

Cora grimaced. "'Wow' was not the response I was hoping for."

"You were hoping for a denial?"

"I was hoping for an answer. Preferably an honest answer, but even a lie would be better than 'wow.'"

Crowley exhaled, shook his head. "You're an exhausting woman."

"That's what my ex-husband Frank said. It's one of the reasons he became my ex-husband."

"Is that why you're not married?"

"No. Frank was several husbands ago. Don't change the subject. Look. I've never had a case with you before. I don't know how you work. Letting me go with what you had on me was not exactly by the book. Even my lawyer couldn't understand it, and for a woman who looks like a centerfold, she's pretty damn sharp."

"What's this about someone following you?"

"Someone followed me home, and it wasn't a stray puppy dog."

"Who was it?"

"Still acting like it wasn't you? Interesting."

"If someone's following you, I'd like to know."

"Why?"

"Don't be silly. It could be a lead."

"And you have so few."

Crowley exhaled through his teeth. It occurred to Cora he could use some dental work. "I let you go because I don't want to waste my time on you. I got a murder to solve. You didn't kill the guy. You had no reason, and with your lawyer making a stink about the ballistics evidence, it's a cinch the bullet isn't going to match. On the other hand, if someone's taking an interest in you, it's something I should know."

"You've almost got me convinced it isn't you."

"You want me to take a polygraph?"

Cora smiled. "That could be a pretty good bluff."

"I told you. I don't bluff."

"Just what someone bluffing would say."

Crowley waggled his fingers next to his temples. "Snakes. You got snakes in your head. Okay, lady. You say you're being followed. You got anything concrete to go on? I don't suppose you got the plate?"

"As a matter of fact, I do."

Cora took out the license plate number, passed it over.

"This is a Connecticut plate," Crowley said.

"Sorry. I know you can't trace them."

"Yeah." Crowley snatched up the phone. "Perkins. Trace a license for me. Connecticut plate, number two, seven, nine, three, eight." He hung up with a flourish.

"Showoff," Cora said. "You're saying you *can* trace a Connecticut plate?"

Crowley shrugged. "Just routine."

"Oh, yeah? Bet you fifty bucks you can't trace that plate."

"I don't want to take your money."

Cora nodded. "I understand. Little much on a sergeant's salary."

Crowley exhaled again. "You're on, lady."

They shook hands.

The phone rang.

"Fast enough for you?" Crowley said. He scooped it up. "Okay, Perkins, what you got?" The smile froze on his face. "Run that by me again." He listened, said, "Double check it. . . . No. I'm sure you did. Do it again." He hung up the phone.

Cora cocked her head, smiled. "Earful of cider?"

Crowley scowled. "What?"

"Never saw *Guys and Dolls*? Sky Masterson tells Nathan Detroit what his father told him to do if a man ever offered to wager he could make the jack of spades jump up out of the deck and squirt cider in his ear: 'Do not bet this man, my son, or you will wind up with an earful of cider.'"

Once more, Crowley let out a breath. Cora could practically see steam. "I got hustled."

"Big-time. At least you're quick on the uptake."

Crowley looked pained. "You going to make me pay off a sucker bet?"

"They're the only ones I make."

The sergeant whipped out a billfold. He made sure Cora couldn't see how much was in it while he took out a ten and two twenties.

Cora stuck the bills in her purse. "The plate's unregistered. To get your fifty bucks back, tell me who issues unregistered plates."

"Love to. Can't do it."

"Why not?"

"No one does. Do I win the bet?"

"What bet? I didn't bet you. I offered money for service. You can't provide the service."

Crowley leaned back in his desk chair, studied Cora thoughtfully. "I don't know why you're torturing me. I let you go."

"Yes, you did. But I know damn well you're ready to arrest me again on the slightest provocation."

"I ought to arrest you for gambling."

Cora grinned. "Oh, that would look good in court. I can just hear you on the witness stand explaining how it happened."

"While you're in such a good mood, I wonder if you'd mind taking a look at the crossword puzzle?"

"Why? No one could solve it?"

"Oh, they solved it. They just couldn't make anything out of it."

"Then I probably won't. Go ahead. Pass it over."

Sergeant Crowley opened his desk drawer, pulled out a piece of paper, and handed it to Cora.

"I can touch it?"

"It's a copy."

Cora scanned the puzzle:

Need a clue?
Here you go
Inner five
Center row.

She shrugged. "Perfectly straightforward, Sergeant."
"What does it mean?"

"Clearly it's referring to a sudoku."

"A what?"

"You mean you didn't find it? Unbelievable. A clue like that screaming for attention."

Crowley practically ground his teeth. "Look, lady. You're good at what you do. Believe it or not, we're good at what *we* do. That does not include interpreting enigmatic clues from crossword puzzles."

"Enigmatic? Wow. You're lucky you made sergeant, talking like that. Most cops say 'enigmatic' get assigned to a desk."

"Are you having a good time? I'm not. I would imagine in that small town you live in—"

"Bakerhaven."

"I would imagine you don't have more than one crime at a time. Here it's a little different. I got dozens. You know which one has priority? They all do. So you'll pardon me if I don't get all excited when you mention some suduko."

"Sudoku."

"Whatever. You wanna enlighten me on the subject?"

"Sure, Sergeant. I will try not to take offense at the fact you have never heard of my line of sudoku books. They're puzzles. If you happen to have two or three hours to spare, I might be able to explain a simple one to you."

"You might explain why I should give a damn."

"You said you want to know what the crossword puzzle means. The crossword puzzle is clearly referring to a number puzzle. Specifically, a sudoku, a nine-by-nine number puzzle that is very popular outside the NYPD."

"How does that help?"

"It tells you what you're looking for. Which makes it easier to find."

Crowley gave Cora a hard stare. He snatched up the phone again. "Perkins. You know what a sudoku is? . . . Then find someone who does. Have 'em review the crime scene evidence, see if anything like that turned up in the apartment."

"I can't believe no one would have mentioned it," Cora said.

"Again, your field of expertise, not mine."

"Yeah, but with a crossword puzzle on the body. I'd think it would ring a bell."

"You have a point, or you just trying to rub it in?"

The phone rang. Crowley scooped it up, listened, slammed it down.

"Good news?" Cora chirped.

Crowley made a face. "Perkins spoke to the detective who reviewed the evidence. No puzzle."

"There's gotta be," Cora said. "What about the medical examiner?"

"What about him?"

"Maybe he found something in the clothes."

"He'd have said."

"Even if it didn't seem important?"

Crowley snatched up the phone, had a brief conversation with Perkins, put it down.

Cora's eyes twinkled. She tipped back in her chair. "You married, Sergeant?"

"Why?"

"I wasn't proposing. Just passing the time. Assuming it will take your boy a little while to browbeat the medical examiner."

"That's not the way it works."

"How does it work?"

Crowley looked at her sharply. "What do you care?"

"I'm just a country girl from the sticks, trying to make my way in the big city."

"Didn't you used to be from New York?"

"Where'd you hear that?"

"I don't know. Just seemed like you were."

"Really? I've been in the country so long, I barely remember the city."

"And yet you own an apartment."

"Which is rented. The rental covers the maintenance, brings in pocket change. Win—win. Of course, once a New Yorker, always a New Yorker. Seems like only yesterday, and it's been fifteen years." Cora realized that made her seem old. "I recall I'd just turned twenty," she hastened to add.

Crowley laughed.

"You find that funny?" Cora said.

Crowley shook his head. "Lotta women been married several times before they were twenty. We just booked one. On prostitution. I don't think all her marriages were legal, though."

Cora nodded. "Some of mine weren't either. Since you ducked the question, I assume you're married."

The phone rang. Crowley scooped it up, not, Cora noted, without some relief. "Yeah? . . . Really? . . . Well, I'm sure he was. Could you ask him to fax it over? Without handling it any more than he already has. If he's really sorry, tell him I need it *now*."

Crowley hung up the phone. "It'll be right here."

"If the doctor cooperates."

"Perkins has him by the short hairs. He'll cooperate."

He did. Perkins knocked on the door less than five minutes later, handed Crowley the fax.

Crowley held it up for Cora.

	2	6	4				7	1
				7				
1				8			3	
		7					4	2
4						8		6
		3		1				
			3		6	2		
		5			1			9

"I assume this is what you mean?"

"You've never seen a sudoku before?"

"I'm sure I have. I'm sorry it didn't make a big impression. Can you solve it?"

"Just watch me."

Cora whizzed through the sudoku in less time than it took the doctor to send the fax.

She looked at the solution, whistled.

"What is it?"

Cora handed Crowley the sudoku. "Look at the middle row across."

Crowley looked at the sudoku.

8	2	6	4	3	5	9	7	1
5	3	4	1	7	9	6	2	8
1	7	9	6	8	2	4	3	5
9	1	7	5	6	8	3	4	2
4	5	2	7	9	3	8	1	6
6	8	3	2	1	4	5	9	7
2	6	8	9	4	7	1	5	3
7	9	1	3	5	6	2	8	4
3	4	5	8	2	1	7	6	9

"What about it?"

"What are the five numbers in the middle of the row?"

Crowley read them off. "Two, seven, nine, three, eight."

Cora cocked her head at him, smiled. "Ring a bell?"

"No," Crowley said irritably. "What are you getting at?"

"It's the license plate number Perkins couldn't trace."

Chapter

1 6

Becky Baldwin pushed the long blond hair out of her eyes, tapped the pencil against the yellow legal pad on her desk. "What the hell is going on?"

"I have no idea," Cora said.

"But it's all about you. Which makes no sense. But it has to."

"We've been over this before."

"It just *happened*. You just *told* me about it."

"Yeah, but it's the same concept."

"Right. The killing had to do with you. Because of the cross-word puzzle. Which makes no sense, because the killer must have known I was bringing you, but he couldn't. Because *I* didn't know I was bringing you. I just decided it that day."

"Well, that's not quite true, is it?" Cora said.

"What do you mean?"

"You asked me the day before. And then that night I asked Aaron about theater tickets. And he asked around to see if he could get some. Which is how we wound up at the play. So Aaron knew

I was going, and presumably the people he asked knew I was going."

Becky shook her head. "I would hate to have to sell that to a jury."

"Why?"

"The killer invites me to a meeting in New York. Even that's an assumption, but say he does. The killer invites me to a meeting in New York. I decide I'm going to bring you. He finds out I'm bringing you and says, 'Oh, great, the Puzzle Lady, I'll give her a puzzle.' So he devises a crossword puzzle and a sudoku that, taken together, yield the license plate number of the car he's going to use to follow us home."

"Why not?"

"Why not? I'm an editor. I read this in a manuscript, I throw it across the room.

"I mean, come on, give me a break. Not only did the killer decide to work this license plate number into the crossword puzzle once you were involved, but the plate in question is a totally bogus one manufactured specifically for that purpose."

"Well, when you put it like that," Cora said.

"It's enough to make your flesh crawl."

Cora fished a pack of cigarettes out of her purse.

"You can't smoke in here."

"My flesh is crawling. You expect me not to smoke when my flesh is crawling?"

"What did Chief Harper say?"

"I haven't told him."

Becky stared at her. "You haven't told him?"

"It's not his case. It's out of his jurisdiction."

"If a killer's tailing you around town, it's in his jurisdiction."

"We don't know that."

"Of course not. A car with a license plate that matches the clues left at the scene of the murder is probably unrelated to the crime."

Cora lit her cigarette, took a deep drag. "Oh, that feels better."

"Wish I smoked," Becky said.

"Want one?"

"I could use an Ativan."

"That I do not have. Wanna adjourn to the bar at the Country Kitchen?"

"I thought you stopped drinking."

"You look like you could use one."

"I'm all wound up. I'm antsy. You said wait, you had something to tell me, and hung up the phone."

"Well, I couldn't spill it on a pay phone. It would have taken forever. I'd have never got out of New York."

"You could have given me the general idea."

"Right, right. You're an attorney. *You* summarize the situation in one short, pithy sentence."

"So what do the cops think?"

"They think I'm a major pain in the ass, and they wish they'd never heard of me."

"About the case."

"I thought that *was* about the case. As far as the murder's concerned, they have no idea who killed him or why."

"Did he have any enemies?"

"I have no idea."

"I thought you had that sergeant wrapped around your finger."

"What made you think that?"

"I don't know. Just your manner."

"My manner? Not his?"

"What are you asking?"

"Just trying to figure out what you saw."

"I saw you lapse into flirty mode. And the guy did let us go."

"He had good reasons."

"I'm an attorney. You're apprehended at the scene of a shooting with a recently fired gun. Your saying it's not the murder weapon is probably not a unique defense in the annals of crime detection."

"The claim was made by an attorney demanding a ballistics test."

"What's the attorney supposed to do? Claim it's not the murder weapon and *object* to a ballistics test?"

"Yes, but—"

"Cora. All I said was you seem to have worked your feminine wiles on the sergeant, and you flew into more defenses than I raised against the murder charge. Looks like I touched a nerve."

Cora took a deep drag on the cigarette, blew it out again. "Yeah. I guess I'm a little touchy since I broke up with Barney."

"Well, come back to earth and focus on the problem. It would appear a killer followed us home."

"With clearly no intent to do us harm," Cora said.

"Why do you say that?"

"Because he could have. He doesn't want to. He wants to play a game. He wants to play with me, not you. Or he would have left a legal puzzle, not a crossword."

"Not knowing you can't do them."

"Hey. Haven't you gotten enough jabs in?"

"Yeah, yeah. Fine. So what are we going to do about it?"

"Only one thing we can do. Wait and see what happens."

"You don't think we need protection?"

"I've got a gun. I don't think he's after you."

"You don't *think*?"

"Want me to get you a gun?"

"No."

"So just take normal precautions. Don't go out alone after dark."

"Wonderful."

"Hey. I'm not worried." Cora considered, frowned. "Sherry's not going to be happy."

Chapter

1 7

"This is creepy," Sherry said.

"Don't worry. I'm sure you and Jennifer are safe," Cora said, and bit her lip. She knew it was a stupid thing to say the minute the words were out of her mouth.

Sherry immediately picked up the baby. Jennifer, who'd been playing happily on the living room floor, burst into tears at this rude interruption of her fun.

"Now see what you've done," Sherry said.

Cora felt betrayed. *She* hadn't done anything. These young mothers. So wrapped up in their children, they lose all sense of reality. Hell, they lose all sense. Just because a psycho killer was stalking them. Which wasn't even happening, and wasn't likely to happen, which is all she'd been saying, and while she might have worded it better, there was really no call for such a flagrant overreaction.

Which, Cora knew, wasn't really fair to Sherry. Jennifer had already had an experience with such a person, and though she'd been too young to realize it, it had to be uppermost in Sherry's mind.

"For goodness' sakes," Cora said. "I didn't mean to panic you. I was telling you there *wasn't* any danger. It didn't occur to me that would make you think there *was.*"

"You think I'm overreacting?"

"I didn't say that either. The crossword puzzle and the sudoku indicate that someone's playing a game with me. Me, not you. I'm the Puzzle Lady. No one outside the immediate family knows you have anything to do with it. Hell, I haven't even told Jennifer."

"Don't try to humor me."

Cora took a last bite of salmon, put her plate on the floor for Buddy. She'd gotten home to find Sherry had food waiting. She also had food waiting for Aaron, but he was working late at the paper. This was unfortunate. Cora figured Sherry was more anxious than normal because Aaron wasn't there.

Not that the news wasn't alarming anyway. The fact that the killer had targeted Cora in advance was weird. Worse, it seemed next to impossible.

"I don't know how you can be so calm," Sherry said.

"I have a gun."

"Cora."

"Crowley doesn't think I'm in danger."

"Who?"

"The sergeant in charge of the case."

"Oh? It's Crowley, is it?"

"Well, 'the sergeant in charge of the case' is a mouthful." Cora shook her head. "There's no pleasing you."

Sherry got up, went to the window. She pushed the curtain aside and peered out. "There's lights down on the road."

"It's a road. People use it."

"Not so often. We're in the country. There's lights at the foot of the driveway."

Cora blinked. "Are cars *stopping* at the foot of the driveway?"

"No."

"They're just driving by?"

"Slowly."

"How slowly? Like not wanting to miss a turn slowly? Like not wanting to slide off the road slowly? Or like trying to creep you out slowly?"

"Like looking up the driveway slowly."

"Oh? You can see the car?"

"I can tell how fast it's going."

"Oh, for goodness' sakes." Cora got up, went to the window. "Where? Where's this slow car?"

"It went by."

"It drove off. How suspicious. It must have known I was getting up from the couch and wanted to frustrate me."

"It was there. It drove off, and— Jennifer! No!"

The baby had joined Buddy in cleaning up Cora's plate. Buddy was licking it, and Jennifer was mopping it up with her hand.

Sherry rushed over and picked her up. Buddy barked and Jennifer burst into tears.

"I thought you were watching her," Sherry accused.

Cora opened her mouth to protest, realized her niece wasn't rational at the moment. She picked up the plate, which Buddy had pretty well licked clean, and escaped to the kitchen. She put her plate in the sink, tossed Buddy a puppy biscuit, and went back in the living room.

Sherry was jouncing Jennifer on her shoulder and looking out the window. "Here he comes again."

"The same guy? You recognize the headlights?"

The car slowed at the foot of the driveway and turned in.

"Oh, my God!" Sherry said.

"It's just Aaron," Cora said.

"Not from that direction."

"Oh, pooh," Cora said. Still, she grabbed her purse off the coffee table, fumbled for her gun.

Headlights came up the drive.

Cora stepped out on the front stoop, brandishing the gun.

The car pulled into the light. It was a police cruiser.

Dan Finley got out. "You gonna shoot me, Cora?"

"That depends. Why are you here?"

"Chief asked me to check on you."

"Why?"

"I don't know. Didn't you find a body, or something?"

"Yeah. In New York City. What's that got to do with you?"

Dan put up his hand. "Hey. Don't shoot the messenger. Chief asked me to drop by, make sure everything's okay."

"Everything's okay."

Sherry pushed out the door with Jennifer on her hip. "What made him think it wasn't?"

"See?" Cora said. "Now you've upset the young mother."

"Does the chief think we're in any danger?" Sherry persisted.

"No, of course not. He just said to do a drive-by. I'm not sure why. I think he got a call from some cop in New York."

"Who thinks we're in danger," Sherry said.

"He didn't say that. He just said keep an eye out, make sure no one's taking an undue interest in you."

"See?" Sherry said.

Dan opened his mouth, closed it again. Looked totally frustrated.

"It's not your fault," Cora said. "I told her there's no danger, she immediately wanted to know what danger there *wasn't*."

"Apparently there isn't any at all," Dan said. "The only one taking any interest in your house is me."

"You drove by more than once?" Sherry said.

"I sure did. And there is absolutely nothing happening."

"Of course not," Cora said. "The fact is, I was picked up on suspicion of murder. The cops had to let me go, but they're not happy about it, and they'd like to keep an eye on me."

"Are you kidding?"

"I was caught with a smoking gun. The only reason I'm not in jail is I've got a hell of a lawyer."

"Is that true?"

"Of course it is. You wanna call the chief, tell him you did your drive-bys and I seem to be behaving, feel free. Just try not to look like a stalker when you do."

"How am I supposed to do that?"

"I don't know. Put your lights on, or something."

"That'll just scare them away."

"There's no one to scare. Except Sherry. And you're doing a very good job."

Dan shrugged, got back in his car, and drove out the driveway.

"Okay," Cora said. "Can we go back inside, sit down, relax, maybe watch some TV?"

Sherry blew out a breath. "Sure."

Cora went back in the living room and put on the Yankees game, knowing it would drive Sherry away. It was two–two in the top of the sixth, and some Cleveland batter Cora had never heard of kept fouling off pitches.

Cora leaned back on the couch, tried to relax. Despite what she told Sherry, she was pretty wound up. She picked up the remote, flicked through the channels. Couldn't find anything she wanted to watch. Came back to the ball game. The same batter was still up.

Cora went in the kitchen, made herself a cup of coffee. Not that she needed caffeine at the moment, but she needed something comforting. What was it Becky said? An Ativan? Cora'd never had much to do with drugs. At least not since the '60s. She wondered if Barney Nathan would write her a prescription. Least he could do, damn it to hell.

Cora took her coffee back in the living room, was delighted to see the Yankees were now batting and Derek Jeter was up.

Sherry came back. "Okay. I got Jennifer to sleep. What's the story?"

"Two–two, bottom of the sixth, Jeter's up."

"Don't be dumb. Dan Finley. Chief Harper. The New York cop. They all think something's up."

"That's good. They'll keep an eye on us. Not that we need it. It's like carrying an umbrella so it doesn't rain."

Sherry went to the window.

"Are you going to do that all night?" Cora said.

"There's a car again."

"Oh, for Christ's sake."

"Going slow."

"You gotta stop," Cora said. Still, she got up, went to the window.

The car had slowed down at the foot of the drive.

The flashing lights on the top went on.

"How about that," Cora said. "Dan Finley did it."

The cruiser drove on by the driveway. A couple of hundred yards down the road, it turned around and came back. Dan left the lights on until it was out of sight.

Sherry seemed on the verge of saying something. Fortunately, she turned on her heel and stalked off.

Cora went back to the ball game. A commercial was on, so the Yankees hadn't scored.

Cora blamed it on Sherry.

The Yankees were up four–two when Sherry came back. Cora cringed. The Indians had the bases loaded with only one out. Sherry seemed like a bad omen.

"The car's back," Sherry said.

"So what?"

"This time it doesn't have the lights on."

"It didn't last time. Dan didn't switch 'em on until he went by."

"It's been there awhile."

Cora sighed, heaved herself to her feet, went to the window.

The lights drove very slowly by the foot of the driveway, continued on toward town.

"It's Dan Finley. He finished his drive-by, he's headed back to town."

"Without his lights on?"

"He forgot. Or he figured we wouldn't still be looking out the window."

Cora heard the crack of a bat, and the excited voice of the announcer. She turned, looked. The Indians had scored two runs, tying the score, and now had runners on first and third.

Cora took a deep breath, held it for a five-count, blew it out slowly. She turned back to Sherry, said with measured calm, "Relax. Go back to bed. There's nothing to worry about."

Cora believed it. Still, she slept with her gun under her pillow.

She needn't have bothered.

The killer wasn't stalking her that night.

The killer was somewhere else.

Cora pulled up in front of the two-story frame house on East Hampton Street to find Sam Brogan sitting on the stoop. It was two in the morning, and the officer looked unhappy. Of course in Sam's case, that didn't necessarily have anything to do with the hour. Unhappy was Sam's default position.

Sam grunted. "So. They disturbed your sleep, too."

"Yeah," Cora said. "And I'm not even on duty."

"You think I am? I'm on emergency standby. Call comes in, report of a disturbance, sound of breaking glass. Which means I gotta check it out. Guess what? No disturbance, no broken glass."

"There was a dead body," Cora pointed out.

"So? No one reported *that*. I don't get the phone call, I'm still asleep."

"How'd you find it?"

"Front door was open. I'm searching for signs of forced entry. It wasn't forced, but it was open. Gotta check it out."

"How was she killed?"

"What, I'm a medical examiner? She looked dead to me, I called it in. I'm hoping it was natural causes and I can go home."

"Chief said she was murdered."

"I'm not saying she wasn't. Just no reason to say she was. Chief can speak for himself."

"He in there?"

"Yeah."

Cora went in, found Chief Harper standing in the middle of a starkly furnished living room. Though, Cora realized, perhaps *stark* wasn't the right word. It was severe, regimented. It wasn't sparsely furnished, but everything was in its place. The mahogany coffee table boasted two cork coasters in square wooden frames, perfectly lined up against each other in the dead center of the table. The end tables boasted identical lamps on identical doilies. The TV and DVD player on the opposite wall were perfectly centered on the couch, their zappers lined up next to them, instead of conveniently located on the coffee table or end tables.

A woman's body lay facedown in the middle of the rug. She was slightly off-center, which would have bothered her, though probably not so much as the fact she was twisted to the left with her right arm flung out over her head and her left arm crushed underneath her. Her light blue housecoat was scrunched up in back with what appeared to be a pink nightgown poking out beneath it. Cora couldn't see the woman's face, but she had curly red hair.

"Is that who I think it is?"

"I told you on the phone," Harper said. "Mae Hendricks."

"The town clerk?"

"Yes, of course."

"Give me a break. I thought the name was familiar. Like two in the morning I should remember?"

"It's nice to see how seriously you were taking my break-in."

"I talked to a clerk with red hair. She didn't seem a high priority."

"She does now."

"It's a murder?"

"I should think so. Report of an altercation. Occupant found dead."

"But no break-in."

"No report of a break-in."

"Report of broken glass."

"You're right. She shouldn't be dead. What can I tell you?"

"How she was killed would be a start."

"No sign of blood. I'd say she was strangled, smothered, or bludgeoned. There could be a bump under all that red hair."

"Maybe," Cora said.

She went over, knelt by the body, reached out, pushed some of the red curls aside.

"You mind letting me do that?"

Cora looked up.

Dr. Barney Nathan stood in the doorway.

It was a slap in the face. And not just his tone of voice. It was two in the morning, and he was fully dressed in his red bow tie. Just like in the old days, when he was still with his wife and his marriage wasn't in trouble, at least if it was no one knew it, and he never appeared at a crime scene unless fully dressed in his red bow tie.

During his affair with Cora, he had often been disheveled. Flustered. Lovable. A real person. Now he was back with his wife, and had reverted to the role of doctor.

Cora got up with false bravado, trying to pretend it didn't sting. "Yes, of course, Doctor. I forgot touching dead women's hair was your personal field of expertise. Please, be my guest."

Dr. Nathan ignored her, strode across the room, plunked down his medical bag, and bent over the body. He checked for a pulse, felt her forehead.

"She hasn't been dead long. Where's EMS?"

"That's what I was going to ask you," Harper said.

"I don't call emergency. Emergency's called first."

"Any sign of what killed her?"

Before Barney could answer, the EMS unit came in with a gurney.

"You're late," Barney said. "It looks bad when the medical examiner gets to the crime scene ahead of the EMT."

The emergency crew was young, and the tall one with the crew cut wasn't a doormat. "Guy had a stroke. What are we supposed to do?"

"Who had a stroke?" Harper said.

"Zak Guilford."

"Isn't he dead yet?" Barney snapped.

The EMS crew looked at him in surprise. It was an uncharacteristically unprofessional remark for the veteran medical examiner. "You mean she was still alive?" the taller one said.

"I have no idea. Get her to the morgue and I'll take a look."

The EMS crew loaded the body onto the gurney and wheeled it out.

Barney picked up his bag and followed.

"So?" Chief Harper said.

"I'll let you know."

"What's your best guess?"

"Within an hour."

"She was killed within the last hour?"

"I'll let you know within an hour."

Dr. Nathan turned on his heel and left.

Harper watched him go. "Wow." He turned back to Cora. "You and Barney on good terms?"

"It's two in the morning, Chief. Everyone's a little touchy."

"Even so."

"Well, I'm not waiting around an hour for an autopsy," Cora said. "Don't call me when you get it. I'll talk to you in the morning."

"You're going?"

"There's nothing here to do. The body's gone and there's no

clues. If there was a clue, dead or alive that woman would have cleaned it up."

"Cora."

"I'll see you tomorrow."

Cora pushed by him, went out the door.

Sam Brogan was still on the front porch. He opened his mouth to say something grouchy, but Cora strode right on by. She hopped in her car, gunned the motor, and sped off.

Cora managed to get as far as the Mobil station before she pulled off the road and collapsed, weeping, on the steering wheel. She killed the lights, prayed Sam Brogan wouldn't drive by. The car was in the shadows, but even so. Her red Toyota was too distinctive not to be noticed.

Schmuck. That total schmuck. How could he be so heartless? Of course, it was the doctor's first affair and his first marital reconciliation. He had probably eaten enough humble pie in suffering the tortures of atonement to be ready to strangle a nun, let alone the woman who had put him in that position. It was no surprise he was so rude to her, particularly on the job and in the presence of the chief of police.

Even so.

Cora cried herself out. She rolled down the window, lit a cigarette, and sat there smoking.

A car came down the street. She ducked her head and it went on by. She sat up, watched the taillights disappear down the road, and took another drag on her cigarette.

She thought miserably what a pathetic figure of a woman she was, sitting there alone in the dark, hiding from the world and nursing a disgusting vice.

Chapter

19

Cora got up late and drove into town. She got a latte and scone at Cushman's Bake Shop, and wandered down to the police station, munching as she went.

Chief Harper's face fell when she walked in. "You didn't get me one?"

"I thought you had yours by now."

"I finished it."

"What do you want? A muffin? A scone?"

"It's all right."

"No, I'll get you one. What do you want?"

"I can't let you do that."

"Why not?"

"I just can't."

Cora shrugged. "Okay, I'll hold down the office, you go."

Harper shook his head. "Forget it."

"Oh, go on, Chief."

"I can't *have* another muffin," he cried in exasperation.

"How come?"

"I'm on a diet."

Cora looked at him. Grinned. "It's all right if I bring you a muffin, but you can't get it for yourself?"

"I can't keep buying muffins. My wife would kill me. On the other hand, if someone gives me one . . ."

"And you complain about my reasoning," Cora said. She sat down, pulled the top off her latte, took a big gulp. "Ahhh. Life feels good again. Here, Chief, have a sip."

"I can't drink your coffee."

"Oh, don't be such a gentleman."

"I'm not being a gentleman. I can't drink the milk."

"Oh. Bad stomach."

"I didn't have it till you came to town."

"That's hardly fair, Chief. As you pointed out, I've been here since the dawn of time."

"Aw, hell." Harper heaved himself out of his chair, walked out the door. He was back in five minutes with a cup of black coffee and a blueberry muffin. He sat down, leveled his finger at Cora. "You didn't see me eat this."

"Eat what?"

"Atta girl."

Harper took a bite of muffin. "Like to know about our murder?"

"It's a murder?"

"Oh, yeah. Blunt object. Like a lead pipe."

"Professor Plum in the study?"

"Yeah. Someone coshed her over the head. That answers that question. Why she would let a man with a lead pipe into her living room at two in the morning is another matter."

"Maybe the killer put her there."

"Why would he do that?"

"I don't know. Sense of composition? Get her away from the front door?"

"Why?"

"It was open. If she was there, someone might have seen her."

"Wouldn't it have been easier to close the door?"

"Maybe he wanted it open."

"Why?"

"To air the place out for spring cleaning? How the hell should I know?" Cora took a sip of latte. "When was she killed?"

"Like the doc said, within the last hour. At least, that's when she died. She could have been coshed earlier."

"You mean lay there awhile and then died?"

"It's possible."

"While she was waiting for the EMS unit?"

"Don't start with me."

"Just making an observation."

"Yeah, well, you got a newspaper reporter in the family."

"You think I went home last night, woke him up? I haven't even seen him this morning."

"You wouldn't give him a hot tip on that angle of the story?"

"Hadn't occurred to me. Now that you mention it . . ."

"Don't mess with me, Cora. I'm not having a good time here."

"Hadn't noticed."

Harper took a bite of muffin, chewed it around. "Anyway, it's official. She was murdered. So, any thoughts?"

"I think it's a pretty stupid crime."

"You think she was assaulted?"

"Only if the killer had an icepick," Cora said. Harper gave her a look. "No, I don't think she was sexually assaulted. I think she was just killed. It doesn't look like a robbery. Nothing seems to be taken. It seems a rather pointless crime."

"Except she was a witness in the town hall break-in."

"A witness to what? She didn't see anything. She didn't know anything."

"Maybe the killer thought she did."

"Why? What would make him think that?"

"The fact we questioned her."

"That makes no sense at all. The killer finds out we questioned the town clerk, says, 'Gee, I'd better kill her in case she knows something she didn't mention to the police the first time they questioned her that she might mention the second time'? What kind of a person thinks like that?"

"A paranoid killer?" Harper said. "All right, put it like that, it sounds silly."

"No kidding. And, no, I don't think it's connected to the murder in New York."

"How'd you know I was going to ask you that?"

"I know how you think. And, no, I don't think it is, unless there's some crossword puzzle or sudoku you're holding out on me."

"There isn't."

"Then I don't see it. The motive is different. The means of death is different. The location is different. The gender of the victim is different. I can't think of a single similarity except both of the victims are dead."

"They're both connected to you."

Cora stared at the chief. "Excuse *me*?"

"You found the body in New York, and you picked a fight with this woman just the other day."

"Picked a fight?"

"Let's not quibble. The point is, you questioned her in the course of a police investigation. That makes two police investigations you've been involved with. In both cases, one of the participants wound up dead."

"Both of the victims used *toilet paper,* and in each case they wound up dead."

"Your interrogation of the town clerk was quite heated. I practically had to pull you away from her."

"Does that make me a suspect? Should I be calling Becky Baldwin here?"

"You have the right to an attorney. I can't imagine why you would need one."

"Then stop playing up my motive."

"I didn't say it was a motive."

"Well, if you're going to nitpick about the wording."

"Cora. It's me. Calm down. I don't think you killed anyone. I'm just pointing out the way it looks to other people."

"People? You're spreading it around I didn't like the victim?"

"Well, if I'm asked the direct question."

"Who's asking you direct questions?"

"I got a call from Henry Firth."

"Of course you did. He's the prosecutor, he wants someone to prosecute. So, you trotted me out as a suspect?"

"Of course not."

"So what's Ratface got to do with it?"

"Nothing. You just wanted to know who's asking me questions."

"Chief. I asked you if you were telling people about me and the victim. You said if you were asked a direct question. I said who's asking direct questions, you said Ratface."

"I did not say Ratface."

"You said the prosecutor. I asked what did you tell him about me and the town clerk and you said he didn't ask you. *Who* asked you about me and the town clerk?"

"Well, that officer."

"What officer?"

"You know. From New York."

"Sergeant Crowley of the NYPD?" Cora said accusingly. "You called the New York City police department and told them their murder suspect was involved in another murder up here?"

"I didn't call him, he called me."

"Yeah, sure."

"He's worried about you. He said you were being followed."

"So you called Dan Finley and he drove over to our house and scared Sherry silly. So what?"

"He called this morning to ask if there had been any progress."

"And you said no one's trying to kill her, but she's involved in killing someone else?"

"That's not how I phrased it."

"How did you phrase it?"

"I had to tell him I had my own crime to deal with."

"And he asked you if I did it?"

"Of course not. He doesn't think you're a killer."

"What *was* his direct question?"

"He asked if you had anything to do with it."

"That's a paraphrase, Chief. What did the guy *say*?"

Harper took a breath. "'Is that crazy lady involved in yours too?'"

"Nice. So that's the direct question you were referring to."

"I assured him you had nothing to do with it."

"You told him that nutty old bag is innocent?"

"Cora."

"And he asked you if I had any relation with the decedent, and you told him I nearly ripped her face off just last week. I'm surprised he hasn't come looking for me. Oh, that's right. It's out of his jurisdiction. What's the law here, if he wants to haul me in? Would he have to get me extradited?"

"You're making too much of this."

"You trot me out as a murder suspect and *I'm* making too much of it?"

"No one thinks you're a murder suspect."

"Do you have any theories about this crime that *don't* involve me?" Cora said sarcastically.

"Do you?"

That caught Cora up short. "Chief, I don't have any theories about this crime at all. The only thing that makes sense is that it's connected to the break-in, and if you have any idea how, you're way ahead of me. It's kind of like playing a game of no-limit poker with no rules, no time limit, no boundaries, and no purpose. Nothing makes any sense."

"You expect me to disagree?"

"No, but you're the chief of police running the investigation. I expect you know something."

"Can you suggest anything I'm not doing?" Chief Harper said through gritted teeth.

"I don't know. What are you doing?"

"Sam Brogan's searching the victim's house. Dan Finley's searching her office."

"For what?"

"If we knew, we wouldn't have to look."

"How about the murder weapon?"

"We're not even sure what it is. I mean we say lead pipe, but it could be any similar object from a baseball bat to a tire iron."

"Great."

"All that *CSI* crap made popular by television's being done, from searching for skin samples under the fingernails in case she managed to claw her assailant, to analyzing the hairs on her clothes to make sure they're all hers, but just between you and me, I do not expect a solution within sixty minutes including commercials."

"And you're questioning—?"

"My own judgment. I have a feeling nothing I'm doing is worth the time."

"No, I mean who."

"Besides you? The victim's friends. Turns out she didn't have many. Unmarried, lived alone, even her next-door neighbors didn't know her well. Her coworkers didn't like her—go figure—and no one hung out with her. Her parents are deceased, she's got a brother in Oregon who's not rushing to claim the body. She died intestate, not that there's any money anyway, her house was a rental, she didn't seem to own anything valuable."

"So why kill her?"

"Why indeed. It's gotta come back to the break-in, but I can't figure out how. Unless . . ."

"Unless what?"

"Unless it has something to do with the murder in New York."

"How could it?"

"I have no idea."

"Did you suggest this theory to Sergeant Crowley?"

"He suggested it to me."

Cora's eyes blazed. "Oh, did he, now?"

Chapter

2 0

Sergeant Crowley settled back in his desk chair, cocked his head. "I don't see what you're so upset about."

"Oh, really?" Cora said. "You ring up the police chief in my town and, based on no information whatsoever, suggest I might be involved in his murder."

"That's not exactly what I said."

"No, I believe the direct quote was 'Is that crazy lady involved in yours, too?' "

"Oh, that."

"Oh, that? Did you really say 'Oh, that'?"

"It's not like I said you were the perpetrator."

"Well, allow me to commend you on your admirable restraint. How'd you like to be hauled into the police chief's office and asked to explain your nonexistent connection to two murders?"

"Is that what happened?"

"Actually, I wasn't hauled in, I went of my own accord. Because

I wanted to find out if the police had a lead on the murder. I didn't expect it to be me."

"What's your point?"

"You suggested it."

"Because it's there. You can't fault me for saying something that's true. You're like a defense attorney gets all huffy when I call his client armed just 'cause the creep's carrying a gun."

"But he's fine with you calling him a creep?"

"Did you just come in here to bawl me out?"

"Well, it is fun," Cora said, "but I was hoping you would have something to contribute."

"With regard to your crime? I don't know anything about it."

"And yet you accuse me of it to the chief."

"I thought you were done griping about that."

"Whatever gave you that idea?"

"Well, could you get over it? I happen to have work to do."

"Fine," Cora said. "Forget the Connecticut crime. Let's talk NYPD. How you coming with the murder case here?"

"The department frowns on discussing ongoing investigations with murder suspects."

"Right. I'm apt to take something you say out of context, and my clever attorney will use it to beat the rap. And if you think that is a possibility even remotely worth considering, then I despair of you ever solving this crime."

"I'm not too hopeful myself," Crowley said.

Cora stared at him. "What?"

"Evidence is not piling up for me. Usually, you dig into a guy's background, you learn a lot. That is not the case with the late Charles Kessington."

"Oh?"

"The decedent is one of the least interesting people who ever lived. No profession, no skills, and no job. The only thing he had was money, and the only thing he did to get it was have parents who died young. He never married, didn't have a girlfriend, or any close friends at all. He had no hobbies or outside interests that might have thrown him among people. Apparently, his wildest outings were going to the movies or the theater alone. He went to NYU, dropped out when his parents died. Apparently they were the only thing keeping him there."

"How much money did he have?"

"Millions. I don't know how many millions, but I understand it's less than a billion. On the other hand, when you say 'less than a billion,' you're talking about an awful lot of money."

"And that's not a motive right there. Who inherits, for Christ's sake?"

"He has no heirs. No close relations. No valued friends. His money goes to charity."

"You're kidding."

"No. So unless I wanna pin this crime on the American Cancer Society, I'm out of luck."

"He left it all to them?"

"Yes, he did. In a will drawn up by the same lawyer who drew up his parents' wills, who, as you can probably guess, both died of cancer. Now," Crowley said, "the question is, why would a man like that hire the services of an attractive young attorney from out of town?"

Cora shrugged. "You got me."

"Exactly."

She wrinkled up her nose. "Huh?"

"There *are* no other suspects. All I've got is you."

"Oh, come on. Haven't you cleared me by now. When it turned out my gun didn't fire the fatal bullet."

"Funny thing about that."

"You find that funny? What, anything in my favor is just laughable?"

"I mean funny you should mention it. Turns out the ballistics report was inconclusive."

Cora's heart sank. "What?"

"The fatal bullet was badly damaged. Hit bone or something. Bounced around in there. Made a real mess. Anyway, ballistics can't match it up with a bullet fired from your gun. On the other hand, ballistics can't find conclusive proof it *wasn't* fired from your gun."

"You gotta be kidding."

"Hey, these things happen. I'm sure that hotshot attorney of yours will have a fun time cross-examining the expert."

"I'm going to trial?"

"I certainly hope not. But no one's dismissing the charges either."

"You didn't feel this important enough to mention?"

"I think someone's informing your attorney. Has she been trying to get in touch with you?"

"I don't have a cell phone."

"Well, in that case, I'm glad you came in. I was going to call you anyway."

"Why? So you can haul me into court and arraign me, now I can't prove my innocence?"

"No, nothing like that. I've got something I think will interest you."

Crowley pulled open his desk drawer, took out a plastic evidence bag with an envelope in it. "This arrived in the mail this morning." He slid it across the desk. "As you can see, it's addressed to me personally here at the station."

"I assume there was a letter in it?"

"You assume wrong. The only thing in it was this." Crowley pulled out another evidence bag, placed it next to the first.

Cora felt a sense of foreboding. A knot tightened in her stomach. She reached out for the evidence bag, took a look.

It was a crossword puzzle. It had clearly been in the envelope. The creases of the folds were evident. It had been unfolded, but it had not been solved.

Across

1 Ruler deposed in 1979
5 Omar of "House"
9 Risked a citation
13 "King of the road"
14 Scale button
15 Castel Gandolfo's locale
16 Start of a message
18 Put out
19 Cuts one's choppers
20 Hushed up
22 A util.
24 Anonymous Richard
25 Accord signer of 1978
29 More of the message
34 Mr. Munster
36 Horror director Craven
37 Get-up-and-go
38 "Yesterday!"
39 Largish combo
41 Atlantic City diversion

(continued)

(continued)

42 Tattoo word
43 Starting array under "RHE"
44 Oklahoma resident
46 Still more of the message
50 __-face (show of affection)
51 Clampett's find
52 Old Chevy model
54 Doesn't just diet
58 Starchy dessert
63 Can't help but
64 End of the message
66 "Middlemarch" penner
67 English horn's kin
68 Stuff to slog through
69 Station in question
70 Diva Lily
71 13-Across fare

Down

1 Chip, say
2 Fine-tune
3 Up to it
4 Wilhelm in Cooperstown
5 Pal of Lucy
6 Intergalactic distance
7 __-K
8 Goes out with
9 Like chop shop wares
10 Left-handed Fab Four member
11 Ultimatum word
12 Did some batiking
15 Toughie for an ESL student
17 Letter after eta
21 They're sometimes blind
23 Early nickname for Fort Worth
25 SeaWorld performer
26 He wrote of sour grapes
27 Video store aisle
28 Fuse word
30 Jeans name
31 Tandoors, e.g.
32 Course halves
33 Atlanta university
35 Casserole bit
40 Cote call
41 Backyard pond denizen
45 Giraffe's cousin
47 Sewer worker of '50s TV
48 Course chunk
49 Mental picture
53 Still-life vessels
54 Herding dog's name
55 Bunch of bull
56 M __ "mnemonic"
57 Word after whistle or pit
59 Doctrines
60 "Think nothing __!"
61 Medical researcher's goal
62 From square one
65 SHO alternative

"I figure it was meant for you," Crowley said.

"Did it say it was meant for me?"

"Like I said, there was nothing else in the envelope."

"Then you're making a wild assumption. There's no reason to believe it has anything to do with me at all."

"Except the other one did."

"We're not even sure of that."

"It yielded the license plate number of the car that was following you," Crowley pointed out.

"Which is bizarre, but not conclusive."

"Well, maybe this one is. Solve it and let's see."

"You didn't solve it?"

"No."

"You solved the other one."

"Someone solved it for me."

"Why didn't they solve this one?" Cora said.

"I waited for you."

"Weren't you curious?"

"Maybe I wanted to see your face as the answer was revealed."

"Study me for signs of guilt?"

"It's a thought," Crowley said.

"It's a stupid thought."

"Maybe," Crowley said. "But this is a case where I'm looking for someone who makes up crossword puzzles. You're the Puzzle Lady. You make a living making up crossword puzzles. Maybe you make up a set of puzzles that yield a phony license plate number. Maybe before the puzzles are solved, you tell me a car with that license plate number is following you. Then the puzzles are solved, and low and behold, it yields that exact number. Proof positive the killer is following you. Which means, of course, you're not the killer. That's why you wouldn't solve the puzzle for me and insisted I get someone else to solve it. So you'd have time to 'discover' you were being followed."

"That is *so* devious and convoluted," Cora said.

"My point exactly. But that's not going to happen this time.

This time I want you solving the crossword puzzle right here, in my presence. If you created this puzzle, I think I'll be able to tell. You won't be able to solve it the way you normally would, because you'll know all the answers in advance."

Crowley reached in his desk drawer. "So. Here's a copy. Here's a pencil. Prove me wrong."

"I don't think so," Cora said. She stood up.

Crowley stopped her with a gesture. "Not this time. Now that your weapon hasn't cleared, you can either be the cooperating witness to whom I'm extending every courtesy, or you can call your lawyer and we'll take you down and arraign you for murder, and if Blondie's as good as she's cracked up to be, maybe she gets you bail. But maybe not. And this whole spirit of cooperation is off the table."

Crowley shrugged. "You have no options here. You can sit down and solve the puzzle, or you can tell it to the judge."

Cora sat back down. Heaved a huge sigh. "Aw, hell."

She cocked her head. "Buy me lunch?"

"You're a total fraud?"

"Whoa, that's a little harsh," Cora said. At least that's what she intended to say. Her mouth was full of cheeseburger.

Crowley waved his cheeseburger in the air. Grease splattered on his shirt. He took no notice. "You're the Puzzle Lady and you can't do puzzles?"

Cora swallowed the bite, said, "You make it sound like a crime."

"Actually, fraud *is* a crime. Don't you sell breakfast cereal to children?"

"I don't claim it will help them solve puzzles."

"Well, that will be something for the lawyers to sort out. After the parents file suit against the cereal company, and the company turns around and countersues you for defrauding *them*."

"That's not going to happen."

"Why not?"

"Because you're not going to tell them."

"What makes you think I won't?"

"I told you that in confidence."

"You can't confess to a felony and tell me it's in confidence."

"You were talking about a civil suit. Suddenly it's a felony."

"I'm not on the bunko squad. I'm with homicide."

"Exactly. It's none of your business."

"That's not what I meant."

"What's legally binding? What you meant, or what you said?"

"Legally binding? We're just talking here."

"Exactly," Cora said. "We're not taking something someone said and quoting it out of context and threatening them with legal action."

"What's out of context? You said you were a fraud. I said defrauding people is illegal. What am I missing?"

"You're missing the big picture because you're off on a tangent. About a collateral matter that is purely coincidental."

"Does your lawyer know you're a fraud?"

"Why?"

"In her case I'm just curious. I wasn't thinking of charging her with complicity."

Cora looked at him sharply.

He smiled, nibbled a French fry.

"Damn," Cora said. "I can't tell when you're kidding. I'm usually good at that." She picked up a fry. "Becky knows I can't do crossword puzzles. She doesn't know I can't construct them."

"How is that?" Crowley said.

"She knows me as the Puzzle Lady. It came up that I couldn't solve a puzzle. I had to admit that it was very embarrassing for me, but that was the case."

"She still thinks you make 'em up?"

"That's right."

"I'm surprised. That doesn't sound logical to me."

"I told her some constructors can't solve."

"And she bought it?"

"Apparently some can't. There's a rival constructor in town. I told him the same thing and occasionally asked for his help."

"Hmm," Crowley said. "He got the hots for you?"

"What's that got to do with it?"

"Well, if he's got the hots for you, he could be just pretending to believe you."

"Harvey Beerbaum? He's a prissy old fussbudget. Sometimes I think he's gay."

"So he doesn't have the hots for you?"

"Actually, he does."

"See?"

"Anyway, that's the story. You gonna smear me with it, end my career?"

"That's not why I was asking."

"Why were you?"

"Frankly I just want the damn puzzle solved."

"And you can't do it yourself?"

"Look who's talking."

Cora ignored the comment, picked up a greasy French fry. "I must say, I hardly expected you to spring for such a classy establishment."

"Hey. It's close to the office, and you don't need a reservation. So it's not Peter Luger's."

Cora's eyebrows raised at the mention of the most famous steak house in New York City. "You eat at Peter Luger's?"

"If I save up my allowance. And have time to get to Brooklyn."

"You're a sergeant. Don't you make your own time?"

"Yeah, right," Crowley said. "You know how many cases I handle. Some days I'm lucky to get lunch delivered."

"You're out now."

"It's a special case. The beloved Puzzle Lady might be charged with murder. Schoolkids might be disillusioned."

"And you figure if you ply me with cheeseburgers and fries, I just might confess?"

"I wasn't counting on it."

"Then why'd you agree to lunch?"

"I was hungry. And I wanted to see how you were going to squirm out of it."

"What made you think I would?"

"You wouldn't solve the first puzzle, feigned a whopping indifference. I didn't know why, but it seemed worth checking."

"And this helps your investigation how?"

"Well, if it's true, and I don't know why it wouldn't be, it lets you off the hook for creating the puzzles. You have anyone can corroborate the fact you can't construct?"

"My niece Sherry. She actually creates the puzzles."

"And you take credit for them?"

"Hey, it wasn't my idea."

"Then why do you do it?"

"At the time, she was hiding from an abusive ex-husband. I was glad to do it for her. I didn't realize I was condemning myself to a lifetime of pretense."

"The ex-husband still a problem?"

"Haven't heard from him lately. He got married, which didn't slow him down any. Then she got married and had a kid. I think he's starting to get the hint."

"Any chance he could be behind this?"

"No."

"How do you know?"

"Wouldn't have the nerve. Oh, he's not above sending a few threatening puzzles. But he's not capable of murder."

"If you say so."

"Oh, yeah. Don't waste your time."

"But you say he could have made up the crossword puzzle?"

"A *blind chimpanzee* could have made up the crossword puzzle. Probably the only person in America who couldn't have made it up is me."

"Well, maybe we'll know more when we solve it."

Cora picked up her cheeseburger. "Maybe so, but neither one of us is going to do it."

Crowley looked around the diner. "There must be someone here can solve puzzles."

"Whoa!" Cora said. "You can't ask a stranger."

"I'm a cop. I can do what I want."

"Where's a *New York Post* reporter when you need one?" Cora laid out the headline with her hand: 'Arrogant Police Officer Boasts, 'I'm a Cop, I Can Do What I Want.' "

"Oh. There's a guy with a crossword puzzle."

Crowley started to get up.

Cora grabbed him by the sleeve. "Hang on."

Crowley looked at her in surprise.

"You can't ask him to solve this for you."

"Why not?"

"I'm on television. My picture is in over two hundred daily newspapers. You can't have lunch with the Puzzle Lady and ask someone else to solve your puzzle."

Crowley sat down. Frowned. "That's a pain in the ass."

"You have no idea."

Chapter

2 2

Cora paced nervously outside the Supreme Court building, often seen in courtroom movies on account of being more cinematic than the Criminal Court building up the street. The Supreme Court building boasted a high, wide marble staircase and huge marble pillars set just far enough back from the street to provide a good camera angle and look imposing as hell. Cora recalled Al Pacino playing a scene there in the movie *And Justice for All*. It occurred to her that was a hell of a long time ago.

Crowley had been gone for half an hour. How long did it take to solve a damn crossword puzzle, anyway? Hell, Harvey Beerbaum would have whipped through it in under five minutes. Sherry, too, for that matter. Clearly cops weren't as smart as they were cracked up to be.

About five minutes later, Crowley came skipping up the street waving the crossword like a giddy schoolboy who just aced his term paper.

"Well, that took forever," Cora said.

"Yeah. The guys who do puzzles were gone. A bunch of us worked on this. I hope it's right."

"You're not sure?"

"How the hell should I know? There's no answer grid to check."

"All the words have to intersect."

"Oooh, listen to the expert."

"Let's get out of here."

"What are you so nervous about?"

"Same as in the restaurant. If one of your cops sees us, I don't want him thinking, 'Why is the chief having me solve the puzzle when he's meeting the Puzzle Lady?'"

"Come on. I wanted to have it solved so I could spring it on you. Not give you time to think while you solve it yourself."

"Even so."

They walked down to Chambers Street, Cora ignoring Crowley pressing the puzzle on her, urging her to take a look.

"What are you so excited about? Do you think it's a clue?"

"It looks like it, but I can't figure it out. I bet you could."

"Do you really think so, or are you just pretending to because you have the hots for me?"

"I really believe it."

"Well," Cora said. "That's not particularly flattering."

"Huh?"

"Oh, dear. I hope you're better at your job than you are at picking up social cues."

"Social cues? Lady, I got a homicide to deal with. I went out on a limb letting my prime suspect go. What more do you want from me?"

The question caught Cora up short. She figured she was blushing, was glad she was walking right along. "Is there a coffee shop around here?"

"We just ate."

"Someplace we could sit."

"How about a park bench?"

"How romantic," Cora said. "I haven't sat in the park with a boy in years."

"That's not what I meant."

"Of course not. I don't even know if you're married."

"What's that got to do with it?"

"Not much. At least that's what married men seem to think."

"You meet a lot of married men?"

"They aren't always married."

"What do you mean?"

"Sometimes they start married, get divorced."

"Because of you?"

"Not according to my attorney."

"You're funny," Crowley said. "Let's go."

"What about the park bench?" Cora said, but Crowley was already escaping down the street.

They found a coffee shop on Chambers, slid into a booth.

"I'm buying," Cora said. "What'll you have?"

"Black, no sugar."

"What a surprise."

Cora gave the waiter the order.

"Now," Crowley said, "you've stalled long enough. Would you care to take a look at this puzzle? Or does someone else solve crime for you, and you just take credit for it?"

"Nice. You really know how to stick the needle in. Here, give me the puzzle."

The waiter delivered their coffee while Cora studied the puzzle. When he left, she read the theme answer.

Only three
Column one
Up and down
This is fun.

She looked up from the puzzle. "You can't figure this out? How could you possibly not figure this out? The way I see it, it's just like the first puzzle. It's referring to three numbers in the first column."

"That would seem obvious. And look at 69 Across: 'Station in question.'"

"What about it?"

"You tell me."

Cora looked at the puzzle. "69 Across: 'Station in question.' And the answer is . . . Penn. Penn Station is the station in question."

"And the question is, what do the numbers in the first column of the sudoku refer to? And that's mighty interesting."

"Why."

"Here's the sudoku we found on the dead man." Crowley pulled it out, set it on the table. "There's three sets of three numbers in the first column. 851, 946, and 273. So you figure it's one of those. But what is it? A train? No, and even if it was, it wouldn't be staying in Penn Station. It might be stopping in every now and then, but it's hardly a number in Penn Station."

"So what is?"

"There's a bank of lockers in the Long Island Rail Road section. One of my detectives thought he remembered they were numbered starting at one hundred and going on up."

Cora shook her head. "Huh-uh."

"Why not?"

"If that's the answer, what's up and down?"

"Aside from the locker numbers, they also have three-digit combination numbers. So we figured maybe up is the locker and down is the combination lock, or vice versa."

"So go to Penn Station and try both combinations on your three sets of lockers."

Crowley smiled sheepishly. "Well, actually . . ."

Cora's eyes narrowed. Her glare could have wilted flowers. "'Well, actually'? Did you just say, 'Well, actually'?"

Crowley squirmed miserably. "My boy Perkins ran up there and checked it out. The locker numbers don't go any higher than the four hundreds. That knocks out the middle three, 946 and 649. It also knocks out 851. Which leaves 158, 273, and 372. None of those combinations work on any of those lockers."

"Well," Cora said. "That's what took you so long. It wasn't doing the puzzle. You were checking it out behind my back."

"It wasn't behind your back."

"It wasn't in front of me, either."

"I was only looking for verification. It occurred to me it would be nice to get back to you with it all figured out."

"You wanted to impress me?"

"Yeah."

"But you know I can't do puzzles."

"But you're great at figuring out what they mean. That's all I wanted to do. I don't know what went wrong. By rights, it should have worked."

"I tend to doubt that."

"That's easy to say now that it didn't."

"I'd say that even if you hadn't checked it. I mean, come on, give me a break. You expect me to believe that the sudoku found on the body would also yield the number and combination of a locker in Penn Station? A locker that would have had to have been rented *today*. I mean, these things have a twenty-four-hour limit, don't they? So, the guy devises a sudoku, primes it with the license plate number of the car he's going to follow me in, and at the same time includes the combination *and* number of a locker he's planning to rent in the future. How the hell does he do that?"

"He could have rented it for twenty-four hours and kept renewing it."

"What, is he nuts? Some of these puzzle people are, they'll jump through hoops just to construct something no one's ever done before. Which I guess will happen until someone designs a crossword with no black squares whatsoever." Cora put up her hand. "Don't look at me like that. I heard someone talking about it. The point is, for all practical purposes, it can't be done." Cora cocked her head at him. "You know what that means, for all practical purposes?"

"Yes, of course."

"I'll tell you anyway. Here's my favorite illustration: A naked man and a naked woman start from opposite sides of a room. They approach each other according to the following rules. They cross exactly half the distance they are from each other and then stop. Then they cross half the remaining distance and then stop. They continue to move toward each other in this fashion. Since the distance between them always diminishes by half, in *theory* they will never meet. Nonetheless, they will soon be close enough for all practical purposes."

Sergeant Crowley grinned. "Are you sure you're the Puzzle Lady? That doesn't seem like an appropriate bedtime story for schoolchildren."

"I didn't always hawk breakfast cereal. I used to have a life. Anyway, you get the point. The chance this sudoku has anything to do with this crossword puzzle is infinitesimal. It has to be referring to something else. You're sure the crossword puzzle was the only thing in the envelope?"

"We were really hoping for a note. But we weren't so obsessed with it we would have ignored anything else."

"No need to get huffy." Cora picked up the sudoku. "I wouldn't have even mentioned it if you hadn't ignored this until I suggested you look."

"Oh, low blow."

"Sorry. I guess I'm a little touchy you keep ignoring my suggestive comments. I've been feeling a little old lately."

"Suggestive comments?"

"Oh, dear. You're not disinterested, just oblivious. I'm not sure which is worse."

"What are you talking about?"

"Well, it ain't puzzles." Cora shook her head, took a sip of cappuccino.

"Sergeant Crowley?"

Crowley and Cora looked up in surprise.

The waiter stood by the table.

"Yeah?" Crowley said.

"I have a message for you."

"Oh? What is it?"

The waiter handed him an envelope.

"What the hell," Crowley said.

Cora leaned over to see.

On the envelope was handwritten in capital letters: TO SERGEANT CROWLEY. (THIRD BOOTH ON THE LEFT)

Crowley flipped it over. It wasn't sealed. He reached in, pulled out a sheet of paper. Unfolded it.

It was a sudoku.

1			6					
							7	5
	2	7	4					6
4				2		3		7
9				5			4	2
5			7					
7	6	3		8				
		9		4				
		5			7		3	

"It was a kid."

"What kid?"

"I don't know," the waiter said. "Some kid left it on the counter."

"Did you see him?" Crowley said.

"Yeah, but I wasn't paying any attention. It wasn't for me."

"Did he speak to the cashier?"

"You'll have to ask him."

"Same one that's on now?"

"Should be. Shift hasn't changed."

Cora got up. "Let's go."

"You want your check?"

"Up front," Crowley said, and hurried to catch up.

Cora was already cross-examining the cashier, who was old, set in his ways, did not take kindly to the suggestion he should have been more observant. "Just a kid. He left the letter on the counter and went out."

"What did he look like?" Cora said.

"A kid."

"How old was he?"

"We don't sell alcohol. I didn't card him."

Crowley flashed his badge. "It's a police matter, buster. Perhaps you could cooperate."

"I could if I knew anything."

"You could give me a better guess at his age. Was he twelve? Was he twenty?"

"He was grown. Aside from that, I couldn't say."

"Could he have been twenty-five?"

"Sure."

"Did he say anything?"

"If he did, I didn't hear it. As far as I know, he just put the letter on the counter and left."

"What was he wearing?"

"I didn't notice."

"Was he naked?" Cora said.

The cashier rolled his eyes. What an idiot. "Of course not."

"How could you tell?"

He blinked. Considered. "Good point. He was probably wearing something like jeans and a T-shirt."

"Any logo on the T-shirt?"

"Hey, I'm not even sure it was a T-shirt."

Cora turned to Crowley. "That's all we're going to get. Let's go."

"Where?"

"Penn Station. Come on."

Cora went out the front door. The cashier tapped his finger on the bill. By the time Crowley paid, Cora was in the street, trying to hail a cab.

"Forget it. I have my police car."

"You don't have it here."

"No problem." Crowley whipped out his cell phone. "Perkins. I need my car."

"A cab would be faster," Cora said.

"Like hell. I can use my siren, go through lights."

"Really? This isn't high-speed pursuit. We're just going to the train station."

"On the other hand, maybe we're racing the guy there."

"While we're waiting, I'll solve the sudoku." She whipped out the puzzle. "I need something hard," she muttered.

"I beg your pardon?"

"To write on. My God, you miss a million double entendres and come up with that."

"Huh?"

Cora fished a section of the *New York Times* out of a trash can on the corner, leaned against a parked car, and attacked the sudoku.

Crowley watched in amazement. "You got all those numbers already?"

"They're easy. I'm working on the hard ones."

"What are the hard ones?"

"The ones I can't solve with you talking to me."

Crowley shut up and let her concentrate.

Cora whizzed through the rest of the sudoku.

1	5	8	6	7	2	4	9	3
6	9	4	8	3	1	2	7	5
3	2	7	4	9	5	8	1	6
4	8	1	9	2	6	3	5	7
9	7	6	3	5	8	1	4	2
5	3	2	7	1	4	6	8	9
7	6	3	1	8	9	5	2	4
2	1	9	5	4	3	7	6	8
8	4	5	2	6	7	9	3	1

"Okay, what have we got?" Crowley said.

"More locker numbers and more combinations."

"If that's what it is."

"Hey, I don't give guarantees. I just solve sudoku."

"Isn't it 'sudokus'?"

"No, it's the singular plural."

"What?"

"Like deer. You can have one deer or three deer."

"You mean like, 'dear, dear, dear'?" Crowley said, shaking his head.

"Serves me right for picking that example," Cora said.

"Huh?"

Perkins drove up in Crowley's car. "What's up, Sarge?"

"Back to Penn Station. Looks like we were wrong."

"Want me to come?"

"No. Hold down the fort."

Crowley and Cora hopped into the car.

Perkins watched them go. He seemed miffed Cora got to go and he didn't.

"Shouldn't we have brought him along to wait in the car?" Cora said.

"Why?"

"So you wouldn't have to park it."

"You're kidding, right?" Crowley said.

Crowley drove up in front of Penn Station and left the car in a bus stop, next to a fireplug, blocking a crosswalk.

"Handy being a cop," Cora said as they walked to the station.

"It does have its perks. Doesn't get me on TV, though."

They went through the main entrance to Madison Square Garden, which shared the space with the station below. Cora recalled when it was renovated in the '60s, creating chaos and inspiring wags to intone, "Lead us not into Penn Station."

"Well, there's the ticket windows," Cora said. "Where's the lockers?"

"Around the back."

"I thought lockers went out after 9/11."

"Suitcase size did. These are smaller."

"How much smaller?"

"Too small to hold a bomb."

"Then what good are they?"

"Thinking of blowing something up?"

"Seriously."

"Stash your ticket. Passport. Emergency cash in case you get mugged."

"Wow. That'll bring in the tourists. You should market that as a sales pitch."

They found a bank of lockers around the back next to the men's room.

"Do you suppose there's another bank of lockers near the ladies'?" Cora said.

"Not if Perkins wants to keep his job. He's the one who said the numbers didn't go up that high."

"Well, if he's right, we don't have many possibilities." Cora pointed to the sudoku. "Just 163 and 361."

Crowley frowned. "Wait a minute. 728's a washout, and 594, but what about 495?"

Cora shook her head. "It won't be. You're looking at the solved puzzle. But 4, 9, and 5 are all given to you as part of the puzzle. This guy's not going to give us the answer without making us solve the damn thing."

"Maybe. But if 163 and 361 don't work, we'll have to try it."

"Let's hope not."

They found locker 163. Cora tried the combination 361 on it. She pulled at the locker door, shook her head.

"Nope. That's not it. Let's try the other way around. Where's locker 361?"

Locker 361 was in the second row from the bottom. Cora tried its number in reverse.

The locker clicked open.

"Bingo!"

Cora reached in, pulled out an envelope. "Uh oh. If there's a crossword in here, I'm going to flip out."

"You and me both," Crowley said. "But I'll bet you it is."

It wasn't.

It was a single sheet of paper with two typewritten words:

Having fun?

Chief Harper was surprised to see Becky Baldwin's car in the driveway. Cora's car wasn't there. It occurred to him Sherry must be using it. Only Aaron's car wasn't there either, and they wouldn't leave Jennifer alone. Could Becky Baldwin be babysitting? That seemed unlikely. The chief couldn't imagine the fashion model attorney burping a baby, let alone changing a diaper. Unless Cora was in charge, an even more bizarre concept. It simply didn't compute.

Sherry answered the door. "Hi, Chief, we're just having dessert and coffee. Care for a cup?"

She ushered him into the living room, where the baby was crawling on the rug with a number of plastic toys strewn around her. Becky sat on the couch with a cup of coffee and what appeared to be a piece of pecan pie on the table.

"Where's Cora?" Harper said.

"Good question," Sherry said. "I was hoping you'd know. How about it? A piece of pecan pie?"

"It's very good," Becky said.

"I try to avoid sweets, but I have a weakness for pecan pie."

"So whaddaya say?"

"I'm on a diet."

"If I can blow my diet, you can," Becky said.

"Fine, fine," Harper said. "Gimme some pie. Where's Cora? I've been trying to call her all day, but the line's been busy."

"Jennifer knocked the phone off the hook. I didn't realize it until Becky came over. Jennifer doesn't do things like that, but she's got a sore throat and she's cranky."

"Not cranky!" Jennifer said. She punctuated the statement by hurling a plastic pig.

"Cora hasn't been home?" Harper persisted.

"You didn't see her? I thought she was going to see you."

"That was a long time ago. She took off, and I haven't seen her since."

"I haven't either," Becky said. "I couldn't get through. I finally came over."

"Damn," Harper said. He noticed the baby, said, "Excuse me."

"You forget who she lives with, Chief. She's heard worse."

"You've got no idea where she is?"

"She doesn't have a cell phone. Why are you looking for her?"

"Oh. We got the autopsy report on Mae Hendricks. Nothing urgent about it, but when I couldn't reach her I got worried. She was being followed. Not that I think there's any real danger," Harper hastened to add.

"Thanks for the reassurance, I feel much better now," Sherry said ironically. She ducked into the kitchen to get the chief some pie.

Becky looked up from the couch. "You worried?"

"Of course I'm worried. Are you?"

"You think I'm over here eating pecan pie for my figure?" She shook her head. "Cora has no sense of restraint. Hell, Cora has no sense. You tell her something's dangerous, she takes it as an invitation to plunge right in."

Sherry came back from the kitchen with a slice of pie and a cup of coffee. "Sit down, Chief. Milk and sugar's on the coffee table."

Harper sat down next to Becky, sipped his coffee.

"What *did* the autopsy say?" Becky asked.

"If I tell you, you promise not to cross-examine me about it in court?"

"How can I do that?"

"I'm kidding. The autopsy showed what we already know. She was killed by a blow to the back of the head, most likely between the hours of twelve and one."

"Based on what?"

"Based on a bunch of factors you can cross-examine Barney Nathan on. That's the saving grace here. It wouldn't surprise me if they included stomach contents and temperature of the body, but that's not my department, I don't have to defend it."

The phone rang.

Sherry went into the kitchen, grabbed the receiver off the wall. "Cora!" she said. With the long cord, she stepped back into the living room. "Everybody's looking for you."

"Is that Cora? I wanna talk to her," Harper said.

"Me, too," Becky said.

"The phone was off the hook. Jennifer knocked it over."

"I wanna talk to her," Harper said.

"Yeah, that's the chief. Becky's here, too. They came over when they couldn't get through." Sherry looked up from the phone. "Cora says hello."

"Let me talk to her."

"Let *me* talk to her."

"We were worried. After all, you were being followed. . . . Really? . . . Are you sure *we're* safe?"

"What happened to her?" Harper said.

Sherry waved her hand. "I can't hear. Everybody's talking at me. How do you know? . . . Oh, that's not good."

"What's not good?" Becky said.

"Okay, I'll tell them."

Harper heaved himself to his feet. "Gimme that." He snatched the phone out of Sherry's hand. "Hello? Cora? . . . Cora?"

"She hung up," Sherry said.

"What do you mean, 'that's not good'? Damn it, Sherry. What is going on?"

"She's in New York. The guy's following her *there*."

Harper made a face. "Oh, that's not good."

"See?"

"Is she coming home?" Becky said.

"No."

"Why not?" Harper said.

"She's under police protection."

Cora hung up the phone, scrunched back under the sheet.

"Who was that?" Crowley said. He put his arm around her shoulders, pulled her onto his chest.

"That was my niece. My lawyer and the chief of police were there, too."

"Popular girl."

"I really appreciate the special consideration, Sergeant. Or are you this cordial with all your murder suspects?"

"You do have a way with words, don't you?"

"Yes and no."

"Right. Good thing the last message wasn't a puzzle."

"Yeah. Funny about that."

"What do you mean?"

"Almost as if he knew."

Crowley frowned. "I don't get you."

"As if the killer was taunting me with the knowledge I can't do puzzles."

"How would he know that?"

"I don't know. That's what's scary."

"The whole thing's scary. I get a message in a coffee shop. The one we went to on the spur of the moment. That means he was right there following us."

"I got the implication, Sergeant. I'm not good with puzzles, but simple deductions aren't beyond me."

"The point is, if he followed us there, he probably followed us here."

"You're a cop. I assume you have police locks."

"The apartment's secure. Just stay away from the windows with the fire escape."

"Which ones are those?"

"The living room."

"So far we haven't needed the living room." Cora traced a pattern on the sergeant's chest. "I wonder if it was as big a shock for him as it was for me."

"What?"

"Finding out you lived in the West Village."

"Hey, I used to be a hippie."

"You're too young to be a hippie."

"There were hippies in the seventies."

"There was disco in the seventies."

"Even so."

"You have a bong?"

"What's that got to do with it?"

"You're the one making the claim."

"I'm a cop. I'm not claiming a bong. I got a Jimi Hendrix poster."

"Oooh. Can I touch you?"

"Silly question."

"Yeah. I like the way you sidestepped my *other* question."

"What question?"

"Standard treatment, or should I consider myself flattered?"

"Don't be silly."

"I'm coming off a bad breakup. A one-night stand isn't out of the question. I just want to know if it is."

"Oh."

"Well. That answers the question."

"Sorry. I never considered."

"Exactly." Cora took a breath. "Don't mean to be a downer. I'm actually having a good time. So, any theories on the case?"

"I would say you're practically exonerated."

"I like your screening process. Glad I passed."

"The killer targeted you. The only question is was he targeting you before the first crime or after?"

"He left puzzles at the first crime."

"Yes, he did."

"And he sent puzzles."

"He sent them to me, not you," Crowley said.

"They were meant for me."

"How do you know?"

Cora frowned. "Wait a minute. What are you saying?"

"Maybe you just happened to be along."

"Oh, give me a break."

"Take this as a premise: He left puzzles for the cops. You walk in on the first crime, scare the killer away. The killer tails you to see what your angle is. He follows you home, gets your address, your license plate, traces 'em, finds out who you are."

"He knew that already."

"That's one theory. We're working on the theory he didn't. What happens next? He sends a puzzle to me—not you, me—because I'm the cop in charge. He sends me a puzzle, tails me when I leave work. Sends me a puzzle in the restaurant."

"Then why is the message in the locker not a puzzle?"

"I can't solve 'em. Last puzzle he gave me I took forever to get it solved. He's tired, he doesn't want to wait around. He says, screw it, I'll just send him the message."

She shook her head. "No good."

"Why not?"

"He had to put the message in the locker before he sent you the puzzle. The one you took so long to solve. The puzzle gives you the number of the locker."

"Actually, the sudoku gives me the number of the locker."

"Huh?"

"He gives me the puzzle first, sending me to a locker. Any locker. Then he figures out what message he wants to send me. He makes up the message, puts it in the locker, then creates a sudoku that gives me the number and combination of that locker."

Cora blinked.

"Couldn't he do that?" Crowley said.

"I don't know."

"Don't you create sudoku? Or does someone do that for you, too?"

"I create my own sudoku. I just never created one to yield three particular numbers in a column."

"Could it be done?"

"It probably could. I just never tried."

"There you are."

"Still doesn't fly," Cora said.

"Why not?"

"He put the message in the locker because you can't solve puzzles. But he still sent you a sudoku."

"Some people can do number puzzles but not word puzzles."

"You say he found out you can't do crosswords by following you and observing you. By the time he observed that, he's already put the message in the locker."

"Suppose he put *another* puzzle in the locker," Crowley said. "While I'm running around trying to solve the puzzle, he realizes I'm going to take forever, so he runs up to Penn Station, takes the puzzle out of the locker, and replaces it with a simple message."

"Oh, my God!" Cora said.

"What?"

"Your mind is more convoluted than mine."

"I take it as a compliment."

"You take it any way you like. It doesn't mean I happen to agree with your logic. It makes a lot more sense he was following me. He sees you present me with the puzzle in the restaurant. When I don't solve it, he says, 'Oh, my God, she can't do it,' and he rushes up to Penn Station and swaps out a simple message."

"But he's still counting on you to solve the sudoku?"

"It's your example. If it works for you, it works for me."

"Maybe," Crowley said. "On the other hand."

"What other hand?"

"How many people are there that know you can't do crosswords but can do sudoku?"

"Oh, come on."

"There's a few, aren't there?"

"Yes, but they're not suspects," Cora said irritably. "That makes even less sense than the other thing you said."

"Why?"

"If they already know that, why do they leave the puzzle to begin with?"

"To let you know it's for you. They know you'll get it solved somehow. When it takes forever, they get impatient and don't want to wait."

"I still don't like it."

"Even so. Who knows you can't do puzzles and can do sudoku?"

"My niece and her husband know I can't make up or solve the puzzles but I make up sudoku. My attorney and the crossword expert in Bakerhaven know I can't solve puzzles, but think I construct them."

"Anyone else?"

"My niece's ex-husband knows the whole schmear. But he hasn't been around in ages."

"That doesn't wipe him out."

"He's not a killer. He's evil enough, but he doesn't have the nerve."

"Could he make up the puzzles?"

"I don't know about sudoku."

"But he could do the crosswords?"

"He's not worth considering."

"But he could do it?"

"This is a very bad tangent, Sergeant," Cora said. She peeked under the sheet. "I think I'll have to distract you."

He tousled her hair. Smiled. "Distract away."

Chapter

2 6

Sherry's eyes snapped open in the middle of the night. Aaron was snoring loudly. There was no sound over the baby monitor, so Jennifer was sleeping. There was no other sound.

Sherry's eyes flicked around the room. The digital clock said *3:30*. The little moonlight peeking through the edge of the curtains was enough to assure her there was no one in the room. And yet something had woken her up.

Sherry swung her legs over the side of the bed, padded barefoot to the door. She opened it, peered down the hall. It was dark except for the night-light in front of Jennifer's room. The door was ajar, just the way she'd left it. Everything was fine. Still Sherry tiptoed down the hall, pushed Jennifer's door open, and peered in.

The baby stirred, gurgled, turned over.

Sherry stepped back into the hallway and closed the door, leaving it ajar as before.

Had she dreamed she heard something and woken up? Could

dreams do that? Or was she just jumpy because of Cora? Cora wasn't even here. Could Cora have come home? Not at three thirty in the morning. Not if she was under police protection. Even if she was released from police protection, they wouldn't let her drive home.

Sherry went to the window, peered out. Couldn't see Cora's car. Unless it was in the shadows, behind Aaron's, where it couldn't be seen. But why would she park there?

Had she locked the door? The doors to the addition were locked, but what about the door to the main house? Had Cora left it open when she left?

No, what was she thinking of? Becky had been over. And Chief Harper. They'd come in that door. She was the last one in the main house. She'd locked it when she left. Hadn't she? Or had she? Had the news that the killer was in the city made her careless?

Things were coming fast. Things that didn't make sense.

Sherry felt an apprehension she hadn't had since her ex-husband, Dennis, was plaguing her. But he was over that now, happily reconciled with his long-suffering wife, Brenda, and thinking of settling down and raising a family. Even that made Sherry uneasy. She couldn't shake the nagging doubt he was doing it only because she had, in a fierce competition to show that he, too, could move on, find roots, offer stability.

Sherry shook her head to clear it. Good God, she thought angrily. It wasn't fair that Cora's shenanigans could get her in this mindset.

Was Cora really to blame for someone following her? Well, probably. Cora ruffled feathers in one way or another. People always wanted to take her down a peg. A problem, now that she had a family, a baby, something to protect.

Sherry knew rationally that didn't really happen. This was just a delayed reaction to the scare she'd had shortly after Jennifer was born, when a psychopath had seen fit to punish Cora by punishing her. Not the sort of thing that happened in the normal course of events. In *any* course of events. Traumatic, yes, but as the counselors had said, it was important to move past that, see it for what it was, put it in perspective. The image never leaves you, but it doesn't mean that you are likely to be consumed by fire.

Sherry went to the front door. It appeared locked, but unfortunately it was one of those locks that from the inside you couldn't tell. From the inside the knob turned and the door opened whether the door was locked or not. The only way to tell was to open the door and twist the knob from the outside.

Sherry didn't like doing that. It wasn't like in the city, where you could look out a peephole at the person on the stoop. Country doors were solid. Sherry looked out the front window. There was no one on the half of the stoop she could see. That was the problem with the window. It gave you a clear view of anyone to the right of the door, but anyone to the left . . .

Sherry shook her head again angrily. There was no one there. All she had to do was make sure the door was locked so she could go back to sleep. No big deal.

Sherry twisted the knob, pulled the door open. There was no one there. She exhaled, realized she'd been holding her breath. She almost didn't want to try the outside knob. If it was unlocked, she'd never get back to sleep. She'd keep hearing things. She'd probably search the house.

Sherry took another deep breath. Reached out, twisted the knob.

It was locked.

Of course, he could have locked it on his way out.

Stop it! It's locked, it's nothing, go back to sleep.

Sherry was about to close the door when something caught her eye. There was something on the door. Small, rectangular, white. She stepped out on the stoop and looked.

It was an envelope. Taped to the door with masking tape.

Sherry reached up and pulled it down. The masking tape came away easily, was clearly fresh. Of course, it had to be, since it wasn't there when Becky and the chief had come in.

Clutching the envelope, Sherry stepped back inside, slammed the door. Her heart racing, she looked to see what was in the envelope, dreading what it might be. She reached in, pulled it out.

It was a crossword puzzle.

Across

1 Orienteering aids
5 Name in a 1968 Beatles hit
9 Candidate's goal
13 The dark side
14 "Our Gang" assent
15 From The Hague, say
16 Start of a message
18 2004 Democratic Convention keynoter
19 Loosens, in a way
20 More hackneyed
21 Prefix with corn
22 Heavyweight champ dethroned by Braddock
23 Chuckleheads
26 More of the message
31 Smooth, in music
33 Lena of "Chocolat"
34 Prankster's missile

(continued)

(continued)

35 A Monopoly token
36 Martin's comedy cohost
38 Stable newborn
39 Basketball's Jeremy
40 Need ibuprofen
41 Out the wazoo
43 Still more of the message
46 Clump of hair
47 Rock's Cream, e.g.
48 Sharkey's rank
50 "Enough for me"
53 Lopsided defeat
58 Auto registration datum
59 End of the message
60 Virus named for an African river
61 Spy Aldrich
62 Shia or Sunni
63 Pound an Underwood
64 Longish dress
65 Fifth Avenue retailer

Down

1 Beanery handout
2 Bell-ringing cosmetics company
3 Indy crews' spots
4 Venetian blind part
5 Santana with a 2012 no-hitter
6 Perfect place
7 Dental sheets
8 Mr. Potato Head part
9 Outback automaker
10 List-ending abbr.

11 Tippy-top
12 Whaler's adverb
15 Be overfond of
17 Word on U.S. coins
20 Proverb
22 Banjoist Fleck
23 Times Roman typeface feature
24 Feeling of the defeated
25 Pipes-playing god
27 Obeyed the cox
28 "Mad" feature
29 Artichoke part
30 Where the Clintons met
31 Leslie Caron role
32 Prom flower
37 Battleground state of 2012
38 Seasonal ailment
40 Glow in the night sky
42 Bikini or Eniwetok
44 "Becket" star Peter
45 Resounded
49 Cola wars contender
50 Tracy Marrow's rap name
51 Techno musician supposedly
    descended from Herman
    Melville
52 Zero-star fare
53 Teamster's rig
54 More, proverbially
55 Light bulb, in comics
56 Shaving mishap
57 Understands
59 Non-stick spray

Cora got home to find Jennifer chasing Buddy around the living room rug.

"So that's why he didn't come greet me. Looks like Buddy's found a friend."

Sherry looked up from the couch. "If I buy you a cell phone, will you carry it?"

"Hello, how are you, good to see you, too."

"Seriously, Cora. No one can get in touch with you."

"I called in last night."

"You didn't call in this morning."

"I didn't know I had to, Mommy. Don't be mad."

"Call Chief Harper."

"Why?"

Sherry handed Cora the crossword puzzle.

"What's this?"

"That's what Chief Harper wants to know."

"Sherry."

"I found it last night. Three in the morning. Taped to our front door."

"*What?*"

"I'd have called and told you, but of course, no one can."

"The killer was here last night?"

"Apparently."

"You're not worried?"

"I'm worried. Life goes on."

"Why aren't the police here?"

"They were. They got tired of waiting."

"I mean protecting you."

"It isn't me he's after."

"How do you know?"

"Here." Sherry handed Cora a copy of the solved puzzle.

"You solved it?"

"Of course not. The chief doesn't know I can do it. He had Harvey Beerbaum solve it and brought me a copy."

Cora looked at the puzzle.

"See? It ain't me, babe. You're the golden girl."

Cora winced. "Just for future reference, that is a rather insensitive appellation." She skimmed though the puzzle.

Not at home
Are you shy?
If you run
People die.

"See. It's clearly about you."

"Yes." Cora frowned.

"What is it?"

"Nothing."

"You hesitated."

"I was thinking."

"What were you thinking?"

"I don't know."

"How can you not know?"

"I didn't expect to be cross-examined. I'm sure I was thinking something, but your question drove it right out of my mind."

"You were thinking maybe it was Dennis."

"Don't be silly."

"I said it was you. You agreed. Then had a second thought. He was it. It's one of the first things I thought of. It's an instinctive reaction after all I've been through. Dennis has moved on. I believe it. Chief Harper believes it. Otherwise, he'd be here. This is for you. This is the killer talking about you running away from home, not Dennis talking about me running away from *him*."

Cora sat down, looked over the puzzle. "No other clues?"

"Not that I can see. Of course, you're the expert."

"Funny to hear you say that."

"You know what I mean. If you have any brilliant though slightly illogical deductions to make, pray do."

"It's nice to find out how you really think of me."

"Yeah, yeah," Sherry said. "Any ideas?"

They were interrupted by Jennifer laughing hysterically. Buddy was licking her face.

"I think you've got a new babysitter," Cora said.

"Now that's true love," Sherry said.

"Or she's got strained chicken on her face."

"Jennifer doesn't eat strained chicken."

"Strained whatever. She's a sloppier eater than I am. No, I have no ideas, ridiculous or otherwise. As far as I'm concerned, none of this makes sense, and I wish it would go away. But what are the odds of that happening?"

"Well, you better call Chief Harper. He's having a nervous breakdown."

"In front of you?"

"Of course not. He was a prim and proper policeman. But the way he was holding himself together, I got the impression if he doesn't hear from you, he might explode."

"Becky isn't trying to reach me?"

"Actually, she is. But Chief Harper implied if I didn't get you to call him first, I might suddenly find out I had violated several local ordinances in building the addition on the house, and it would have to be torn down."

"That's one hell of an implication."

"The interpretation is mine. The idea was clear."

"Relax. I'll go see them."

"Harper first?"

"Absolutely."

Becky Baldwin shook her head. "That's incredible."

"No kidding."

"Chief Harper doesn't know about this?"

"He knows about the puzzle Sherry got."

"But the puzzle that New York cop got? Penn Station?"

"I'm gonna tell him now."

"He's not going to take it well."

"Yeah, but there's nothing he can arrest me for. Anyway, I've got a lawyer."

"This is incredible. The killer was in New York *and* Bakerhaven last night?"

"Yeah. He's got a car."

"But you weren't home when he hung the envelope on your door."

"No. He said as much in the crossword puzzle."

"Why would he do that?"

"I was under police protection. He didn't like that."

"How were you under police protection? They didn't put you in jail, did they?"

"Nothing like that."

"Well, where were you?"

"In a safe house with an armed guard. Perfectly comfortable, nothing to complain about. Believe me, if there were, I would have you make a stink. I'm not going to put up with any nonsense."

"You didn't mind being under police protection?"

"This guy's weird, I was tired. I didn't feel like driving home in the dark."

"I don't get it," Becky said. "What's this guy's game?"

"When I surprised him in the bedroom, maybe he thought I saw him well enough to identify him."

Becky shook her head again. "He'd already left a puzzle for you on the body."

"If it was for me," Cora said. "Maybe it was for the cop. He sent the other puzzle to him."

"How about the puzzle taped to your door? Was that for the cop, too?"

"That was after I started messing in the case."

Becky sighed. "Why couldn't you have told me this when you called last night?"

"Chief Harper was there. I'd have had to tell him, too."

"You didn't want to tell him?"

"You're my lawyer. I wanted to tell you first."

"You thought you might need legal protection?"

"I don't know what I thought. Things were coming thick and fast. It was pretty damn confusing." Cora pulled a pack of cigarettes out of her purse.

Becky pointed a finger. "If you smoke in here, I'll explode."

Becky didn't explode. The office door did. Chief Harper came through it like a demon from hell about to rip the soul out of an unfortunate sinner.

"I don't believe it!" Harper said. "I don't believe it! I specifically told Sherry to send you to me first!"

"She did, Chief. I needed to consult my attorney."

"You're going to need to consult your doctor," Harper said. "Have you told her about your New York escapades?"

"Whatever do you mean, Chief?"

"I just had a phone call. From the NYPD. Says he was sent a crossword puzzle which he presented to you, and the two of you used it, along with a sudoku sent to you in a coffee shop, for God's sake, to open a locker in Pennsylvania Station, where you received a message from the killer."

"I think your assumption that the message sender is the killer has not been legally established."

"Don't horse around. This is not a joke. I've got a murder on my hands. The New York police have one on theirs. It would appear they are connected."

"Whoa, whoa, whoa!" Becky said. "That is a totally unfounded supposition. Particularly in view of the fact my client has been arrested in one of those homicides. Saying they're connected has unfortunate connotations."

"That's too damn bad," Chief Harper said. It was indicative of his state of agitation that he did not apologize for the expletive. "I got a killer running around tacking puzzles on her door and leaving messages in Penn Station. And don't tell me that's a supposition. If it's not the killer, it's someone with a bizarre imagination mirroring the movements of the killer. Now, without implying anyone's guilt or innocence or even involvement, what the hell do you think it means?"

"Let me get this one, Becky. Chief, I haven't got a clue. Off the record, I would say while not legally binding, it is entirely likely that the killer is the one who left those notes and that I am being personally taunted. What is *not* established—and I don't give a damn about legally binding, I'm talking about from my point of view—I'm not at all convinced that the murder of the town clerk is any way related. Everything about it, from the MO to any possible motive, seems entirely coincidental and not to be inferred."

"You think it's a different killer?"

"Why not? The town hall break-in was a week before the New York murder. If the murder of the town clerk is connected to the break-in—and even that is yet to be established—then the two murders may be two separate matters entirely."

"Did you advance this theory to the New York cop?"

"He's got his own problems, Chief. He's not asking me for advice about yours."

"Yeah, well *I* am," Harper said. "Dan Finley and Sam Brogan have been over every inch of the town clerk's office—and believe me, they weren't too happy about it, particularly Sam—and they couldn't come up with anything, which is too bad, because the woman had nothing of her own anyone might want to steal. And she didn't have close personal friends who might harbor a grudge."

"It's certainly refreshing to hear your views on friendship, Chief."

"Yeah," Harper said. He turned to Becky. "Let me ask you something. When's the last time Dennis checked in."

Becky blinked. "Huh?"

"He's still on probation, isn't he? Doesn't he have to check in with you?"

"Yes, he does. What's your point?"

"When's the last time you saw him?"

"He checked in about a month ago. Seemed pretty stable for him. Wasn't overtly hostile. Didn't go through the how-much-longer-do-I-have-to-put-up-with-this-crap routine."

Harper turned to Cora. "What about you?"

"What *about* me?"

"When's the last time you saw him?"

"Chief, this is a bad idea."

"What's a bad idea?"

"That Dennis is in any way connected to the murders."

"You think Dennis is connected to the murders?"

"No, I think it's idiotic."

"The puzzle on Sherry's door talked about hiding."

"It's my door, too, Chief. And it talked about being not at home. I'm the one who wasn't home."

"Except that the killer knew why you weren't at home when he left the message. You'd just gotten through playing railway station games."

"Oh, for goodness' sake. Tell me, Chief. Is this something the NYPD suggested to you?"

"Why would they do that?"

"Because they don't understand the situation. You know and I know Dennis had nothing to do with it."

"How do I know that?"

"Because you're not an imbecile with a brain the size of a peanut. How do I know the sun's gonna rise in the morning? You wanna start throwing known facts out the window, how you gonna solve anything?"

"Uh huh," Harper said. "Well, if you're convinced the killer's after you, that simplifies *my* life. You won't object to taking precautions."

"Precautions?"

"Yeah. The killer's clearly dividing his time between here and New York. Even if you don't concede he's responsible for the town clerk, you've gotta admit he's tacking notes to your door taunting you. In which case, you are in danger, and protecting you is my job. So . . ."

"I'm not going to like this, am I?"

"Why not? You were under police protection in New York."

"They have facilities. They have personnel."

"So what? It's not like we're putting you up in a safe house. All I'm saying is I want you home before dark."

Cora's eyes widened. "Oh, my God. A curfew. You're giving me a curfew, like I was back in college."

"You had curfews in college?" Becky said.

"I'm making a point. My point is I'm a big girl and I can take care of myself."

"Yeah. And you can do it at home with your door locked, and a landline for the cell phone–impaired. I prefer that to you driving around after dark playing tag with a psychotic killer. And so would you. If the killer really was at your house last night, wouldn't you rather be there, offering your family an armed guard?"

"Didn't they tell you, Chief? Ballistics has my gun."

"Oh, I'm sure you have another."

Cora took a breath. "Fine, Chief. We'll make a deal. I'll honor your curfew, and you stop bugging me about Dennis. Because, believe me, it's the stupidest idea I ever heard."

Cora had been to Brenda Wallenstein's loft on Grand Street only once a long time ago, but that had been enough to make an impression. It was not the type of fashionable loft associated with SoHo now. It was your basic, unfinished sort, rough and ready, a third-floor walk-up single room with the bathtub in the kitchen, if one could call the few appliances scattered at one end a kitchen, and a shower stall on the back wall with a toilet behind. It was the type of establishment Cora would never set foot in unless dating the hottest new folk-rock sensation in the '60s.

After that experience, the liveried doorman at Brenda's Upper East Side apartment was a surprise.

So was Brenda. Cora had never cared much for Sherry's college roommate. Her bubbly good nature toward attractive men always seemed to grate. It was as if the girl were a rival, which was odd, considering the difference in their ages. Of course, her hippie life-style made her seem like a contemporary.

Or perhaps it was the chip on her shoulder. Since marrying Sherry's ex-husband, Dennis, Brenda had become an aggressive bitch, fueled no doubt by her husband's obsession with his ex-wife, Sherry, a wholly unpleasant situation leading to several restraining orders culminating in the probation that required him to check in with Becky Baldwin once a month. Cora was quite sure the court would not have ordered it had they known the scoundrel had hit on Becky, too.

In any event, Cora was not prepared for the smiling pixie who nearly knocked her down.

"Cora! It is so good to see you. I couldn't believe you called. It's been so long."

Cora took a step back. Brenda was a smaller woman, though what the boys in school would call pleasingly plump, and she was animated. Careless curls framed her round, radiant face. Her brown eyes sparkled. Her lips parted in a welcoming smile. She positively glowed, and—

"Oh, my God! You're knocked up!"

Brenda beamed and nodded. "That's right." She pulled her loose smock around her belly. "Five months."

"I don't believe it."

"I hardly believe it myself. Anyway, come in, come in. Let's sit down. I find I like to sit down more and more."

Brenda led Cora into the living room of a tastefully furnished modern apartment and installed her on the couch. Brenda sat opposite in what was obviously her favorite overstuffed chair.

"So, how did it happen?" Cora said.

"The usual way."

"No, I mean, were you trying?"

"Were we ever."

"These nice new digs. Is that because of this?"

"No, we've been here for a while."

"Daddy had a change of heart?"

"Dennis went to work for him."

"I thought he already was working for your father.

Brenda waggled her hand. "There was downtime. He'd feel glum, get back together with the band. Next thing he'd be missing work."

"And he's not?"

"He hasn't been."

"As far as you know."

"As far as my father knows."

"He's on the road for his job?"

"Some. Not so much anymore. Tell me, how's your grandniece?"

"Sherry hasn't told you?"

"I haven't spoken to Sherry in a while."

"How come?"

"Didn't want her to get the wrong idea."

"What's the wrong idea?"

"I'm having a baby just because she did."

"You mean *Dennis* is having a baby just because she did."

"And that's not the case. We were trying before she was."

"Really?"

"At least we were trying before we *knew* she was. I mean, we were trying and then we found out she was pregnant, and that was fine, and then she had the baby, and that was fine. I called her and saw pictures of the kid online, and she even brought her into the city once and we walked to Central Park and that was fine.

"And then I got pregnant and I stopped calling her and she stopped calling me. I guess if you have a kid, you're busy."

Cora frowned. "You've only seen Jennifer once."

"So?"

"You stopped seeing her after you got pregnant. Jennifer's over a year old. You only got pregnant five months ago. You must have stopped seeing her before that."

"Yeah."

"You stopped seeing her *before* you got pregnant."

"No."

"Wanna review the math?"

Brenda took a breath, exhaled. "I got pregnant before. Had a miscarriage. Another reason I didn't want to tell Sherry. I know she was pregnant, lost the baby, blamed Dennis for it. She'd immediately jump to the conclusion. Which is so unfair. I had a miscarriage. It happens."

"But under the circumstances," Cora said, indicating her swollen belly.

For the first time since she'd answered the door, Brenda's face twisted into concern. "I didn't want to talk about it this time. Until we're sure." She shrugged helplessly. "And how many months is sure? We're at five months. Longer than the first time. That was shortly after we found out. Even so. I wouldn't want to do that to Sherry. And I'm superstitious. I wouldn't want to jinx myself."

"Oh, come on."

"You're not superstitious?"

"Only about poker."

Brenda laughed. "You're a hoot, as ever. Want some tea or coffee?"

"You're awfully happy."

"Well, I've got reason."

"Even so."

From the foyer came the sound of the front door slamming shut.

A handsome, clean-cut, well-groomed young man in a smart, stylish suit and tie came in, and the reason for Brenda's rapture was clear. She had a young lover, a suitor ardent enough to have been awarded his own key to the apartment, so that he could come and go at will during the day while her husband was gone.

Cora's smile was smug.

The young man smiled back. "Hello, Cora."

Her mouth fell open. "Dennis?"

"It's not Dennis."

Sergeant Crowley sounded irritated. "Who is this?"

"Well, I like that," Cora said.

"Oh, it's you. I had no idea. No hi, hello, how are ya? I pick up the phone and you say— What did you say?"

"It's not Dennis."

"What's not Dennis?"

"Dennis Pride. Ex-husband of my niece, Sherry. You were wondering if he could have made up the crossword puzzle."

"I was?"

"You asked me about it."

"I did? Yeah, I guess I did. It wasn't a high priority."

"Did you mention it to my chief of police?"

"Why?"

"Because he seems to have got the same idea. I understand he had a phone call from you."

"Right."

"Did you mention Dennis?"

"I may have asked about interested parties. I don't think I used the name Dennis. What's the big deal?"

"The big deal is now Chief Harper's got it in his head, and it's a stupid idea, and I've got to kill it."

"So, kill it."

"How can I kill it if you keep bringing it up?"

"I can't even begin to follow that logic, but I'll play along. Why is it a stupider idea than the last time you told me it was a stupid idea? Aside from the fact your police chief has it."

"That's the point. He pestered me so much, I figured I'd better do something about it. So I went and called on Dennis's current wife."

"How come?"

"He used to beat his first wife. So I wanted to see if he was beating his second."

"He beat his wife?"

"Don't go off on that tangent. The point is I checked him out. She's five months pregnant. They've moved from a grungy loft to an upscale East Side apartment. He's quit his rock band, gone back to work for her father. Cut his hair, cleaned up his act, bought some new clothes. He's gone from the ne'er-do-well son-in-law to the company golden boy. He's being fast-tracked as the next executive vice-president."

"And you know this because?"

"I saw him. He showed up and talked to me. He's a whole different person. I know there are psycho killers who can appear perfectly nice and no one would ever suspect them, but this isn't that. He's relaxed, happy. And he's not kidding himself, either. He's going to a therapist and an anger management group. Granted, it's like the pod people replaced him with a different Dennis, but, hey, I like the pod people."

"Is that what you called me for?"

"Well, I thought you should know."

"Well, now I know."

There was a pause.

"So," Cora said. "Isn't there anything you want to ask me?"

"Like what?"

"Well . . ." She paused again. "I'm in the city."

"Huh?"

"I came in to see Dennis. So, I'm here."

"Good."

"Yes and no."

"What do you mean?"

"I gotta get back."

"Why?"

"I got a curfew."

"What?"

"Chief Harper doesn't want me out after dark."

"You gotta be kidding."

"Hey, it's your fault. You're the one who didn't want me to go home."

"I had ulterior motives."

"I'm glad to hear it. The point is, if the New York police feel I need protective custody, then he does, too."

"You want me to put you under protective custody?"

"No, I gotta be home."

"I don't understand."

"It's the whole damn Dennis bit. The killer tacked a crossword to my door. Chief Harper's got it in his head that it could be meant for Sherry."

"Because she's the real Puzzle Lady?"

"He doesn't know that. He figures it's for her because the killer knew I was in New York but he left the puzzle there anyway. So if she's the target, he wants me there to protect her."

"Oh, for goodness' sake. Can't the cops do it?"

"There's three cops in the whole town. Counting him. They can do drive-bys."

"That's stupid."

"I agree. You wanna call the chief and talk him out of it? Anyway, I gotta be home by dark."

"Too bad."

"Yeah. So, how about it?"

"How about what?"

"Do you do matinees?"

Chapter

31

Cora, dosing contentedly, groped for the phone, pulled the receiver toward her, and rested it on the pillow.

"Couldn't keep from calling me, could you?" she murmured.

"Why shouldn't I call you?" Chief Harper said.

For Cora, who thought it was Crowley, that was a rude awakening. She had a moment of panic, wondering how badly she'd given herself away, but quickly covered. "Hey, I'm home, I'm home, like a good girl. You don't have to check up on me."

"I wasn't checking up on you. There's been another one."

"Another murder?"

"Another break-in."

"At town hall?"

"No."

"You gonna make me play Twenty Questions? What did he break into this time?"

"The police station."

. . .

A rather exasperated Chief Harper was watching Dan Finley photographing his desk. It was clearly a new one for the young officer, who'd never dusted a desk in the police station before.

"I'm getting a lot of fingerprints, Chief, but they're probably yours."

"You contaminating crime scenes again, Chief?" Cora said.

"There you are! You took your time getting here."

"I was in bed."

"This early?"

"I haven't been getting much sleep. Anyway, I'm glad you got your priorities straight."

"What are you talking about?"

"You want me home guarding Sherry. Unless you need my help."

"You didn't have to come."

"And yet you're pissed off I took so long."

Harper glared at Cora. Took a deep breath. "Okay, I deserved that. But it's embarrassing having the police station broken into."

"You're right. Maybe I should call Aaron."

"Don't kid about it." Harper leveled his finger at Dan Finley. "And if you call Rick Reed—"

"I haven't called anyone. Except you."

"Okay, Chief. I didn't really want to get up. You got me down here, what's the story?"

"Someone came in the rear window," Dan said. "Busted the lock, climbed through."

"No one was here?"

"I was on duty. I went out on my rounds. Actually did a drive-by of your house. Drove around town, came back. Wasn't gone more than an hour. The minute I came in, I knew something was wrong."

"How?"

"Door to the holding cells was open. Door to the holding cells is never open. If someone's in there, you don't want to hear them.

If someone *had* been in there, I'd have thought he escaped. Not that we have prisoners escape, but you know what I mean."

"Dan," Harper prompted.

"Anyway, I went and checked, and the lock on the window was broken. He obviously came in here, because the door was open. And the files on the desk were messed up like someone pawed through them. He didn't make a very neat job of it. There were papers on the floor."

"Was anything taken?"

"We don't know," Harper said dryly, "because Dan can't tell what was there."

"Like I'd have memorized the pile of files? Anyway, I'm processing the desk for fingerprints, but it probably won't do any good. Because there weren't any on the busted window. So I figure the ones I find here will be ours."

"Makes sense," Cora said. "Well, Chief, it would seem you have the situation in hand."

"I don't have the situation in hand," Chief Harper said irritably. "I don't even know what the situation is. You'd think this break-in and the one at town hall would be related, but I can't find any evidence of it."

"You checked the files?"

"Of course I checked the files. The first thing I did was check the files. The file on the town hall break-in's still there. So's the file on the murder."

"So that's the way your mind's running."

"Well, isn't yours?"

"It's certainly a valid idea. You sure nothing's missing?"

"Doesn't seem to be."

"Mind if I check?"

"How would you know what's missing? You don't know what's in there."

"Even so."

"Be my guest," Harper said. He pulled open a drawer of the file cabinet, took out a file. "Here's the break-in." Pulled out another. "Here's the murder."

"Pretty thin," Cora observed.

"Thanks a lot."

"I meant it should be easy to see what's missing." Cora flipped open the file on the murder.

"The break-in's more likely," Harper said.

"Yeah, but I'm partial to murder."

Cora flipped through the crime scene photos. They showed her nothing she hadn't seen before.

She pulled out the autopsy report. "Trauma to the head. Blunt object."

"Yeah," Harper said. "Barney agrees with us on this one."

"Uh-huh," Cora said. She kept a straight face, but inwardly she smiled. The mention of the doctor's name didn't cause the same twinge it had before.

Cora picked up the police report. Stopped. Frowned. "That's funny."

"What?" Harper said.

"I've got Dan's police report here."

"Something wrong with my report?" Dan said.

"It's been stapled."

"Dan," Chief Harper said. "Didn't I tell you to paper-clip?"

Dan shrugged. "Sometimes I can't find a paper clip."

"No," Cora said. "It *was* stapled. It's not anymore."

"What do you mean?"

"Someone removed the staple."

Harper stared at her. "Do you mean—?"

Cora nodded. "I'd say this file's been copied."

Becky answered on the second ring. "Hello?"

"Oh, good, you're awake," Cora said.

"Why wouldn't I be awake?"

"I wasn't."

"What?"

"Feel like a drink?"

"What's up?"

"Well, the police station's been broken into."

"*What?*"

"There's a few things I need to catch you up on. Wanna meet me at the Country Kitchen? I'll buy you a drink."

"Oh."

"What's the matter?"

"I was in the middle of a TV show. No matter. I got a DVR. I'll hit record and be right with you."

Becky found Cora at the bar of the Country Kitchen nursing a Coke.

"What'll you have?" Cora said.

"Scotch on the rocks."

"Whoa. What happened to the frozen daiquiri whatever or the crème de ladylike mush?"

"That's for show. For something of this kind, I need a jolt of hard liquor."

"Something of what kind?"

"Didn't you say the police station had been broken into?"

"Oh, that. No problem. I figured out who did it."

"You're kidding! Who?"

"The killer."

"Ooh, pooh."

"Well, that's something, isn't it? It could have been unrelated. I proved it wasn't."

"How did you do that?"

Cora told Becky about the missing staple.

"That's pretty flimsy evidence to hang a deduction on."

"Granted."

Becky shook her head disparagingly. "That's what you brought me out here to tell me?"

"No."

"Well, what then?" Becky took a sip of scotch.

"I'm sleeping with Sergeant Crowley."

Becky did a spit-take. Scotch showered the bar.

The bartender looked over.

"Got a towel?" Cora said. "My friend choked on her drink."

The bartender came over and mopped it up. "You still got some?" he asked Becky. "Can I get you another?"

"I'm fine," Becky said, smiling at him. "It just went down the wrong way." As the bartender retreated, she lowered her voice. "Are you nuts? Are you out of your mind? That's the officer in charge of your case."

"Yeah. I thought it might be a good idea to ingratiate myself."

"Don't make me spit more scotch. A good idea? Do you have any idea how *bad* an idea that is?"

"No, but I'm sure you're going to tell me."

"It's the worst idea ever. Short of confessing to the crime. You didn't do *that,* did you? Just to try to get a rise out of him."

"No pun intended."

"You're hopeless. It's like having a two-year-old for a client."

"Wanna calm down and look at this rationally?"

"Look at what? The case is out the window and you're off on a schoolgirl fling."

"You really need to get out more, Becky. Your intolerance of other people's relationships is an unattractive trait."

Becky chugged the rest of her scotch. "There. I'm out of ammunition. Anything else you wanna surprise me with isn't going to work."

"Good. Here's the situation: I got the inside dope on this crime. The killer is tracking me, *and* he's tracking Sergeant Crowley. He sent us a sudoku while we were in a coffee shop. He could have been following me, but he also sent him a puzzle at the precinct before I even got there. He also tacked a puzzle to my door, and broke into the police station. The killer is a busy little beaver. Considering we haven't got a single thing on him, he's working awful hard."

"So?"

Cora shrugged. "Why? Why is he breaking into town hall and the police station? What does he hope to accomplish? We have no idea. None." She raised her finger. "And we don't even have a viable suspect."

"What do you mean?"

"Normally there would be someone involved in the case. An ex-wife. A girlfriend. A next-door neighbor. A friend."

"A suspect?"

"Not even a suspect. A perfectly ordinary innocent bystander.

Who would turn out to have a secret motive no one would ever suspect. Who is that person in this case? Can you name one?"

"I don't know the dead man's circle of acquaintances. I'm a small-town girl. He's a big shot from New York."

"Exactly. We can't investigate him. And the police *won't* investigate him, because they already have their chief suspect. Me. But that's changing. Crowley and I are working the case together. Not that he's cleared me, or anything."

"You're sleeping with this guy so he'll help you investigate the case?"

"Don't be silly. That's just one of the fringe benefits." Cora shook her head. "You really do need to get into a relationship. Maybe you could lure Dr. Nathan away from his wife again."

"That's not even funny."

"It's a *little* funny. Maybe not spit-your-scotch-on-the-bar funny, but it's a little funny." Cora signaled the bartender. "Another scotch for the young lady."

"You have another revelation planned?" Becky said. "The victim is your secret love child?"

"Oh, *there's* a revelation. The son I never knew I had. That works better with men, though. Women usually know if they've had a child."

"Not you, goosey."

"Well, who then?"

"I don't know. How about Sergeant Crowley?"

Cora's mouth fell open. "Oh, you naughty girl. Paying me back for the Dr. Nathan crack."

"Well, who'd have more reason to humiliate the sergeant than the love child he never acknowledged?"

Cora shook her head. "Crossword puzzle at the crime scene. Prior to Crowley catching the case."

"He's a sergeant. He doesn't catch the case. Another detective does and reports to him."

"Are you seriously considering that as a possibility?"

"No, I'm just pointing out we have no *other* possibilities."

"Except me."

"Wow," Becky said. "Interesting concept. You talk the guy into hiring me, knowing I'll bring you along. On the day of the murder, you drive to New York, kill him, rush back just in time to drive to New York again with me. We get there, go upstairs, find the apartment door open—of which you are well aware, having left it that way. We go in and find the body, with the crossword puzzle you have carefully planted. You pretend you hear something in the bedroom, rush in there, fire a couple of shots out the window, come back, and claim the killer just escaped."

Cora smiled, patted her hand. "Nice try. The doorman called upstairs and spoke to the killer." She cocked her head. "It's not like you to miss a small detail like that."

"Well, you drop a bombshell on me about sleeping with the sergeant."

"What bombshell? It's perfectly foreseeable. Why do you think he let us go in the first place?"

"Oh, listen to you now. As if the thought ever crossed his mind."

"Well, not consciously. But even you couldn't understand why he let us go." Cora changed the subject. "Anyway, I found out something."

"What's that?"

"Dennis isn't guilty."

Cora told Becky about meeting Dennis Pride. She left out the part about Brenda being pregnant.

"I told you he'd cleaned up his act," Becky said.

"I had to see for myself."

"And?"

"I'm totally sold. Not that he didn't do it. I *know* he didn't do it. I mean that he's cleaned up his act."

"How could you tell?"

"He was genuinely glad to see me."

"Whereas most people hate your guts. I can see the logic."

"Hey, I know he's a detestable, conniving son of a bitch, but I tend to believe him. Anyway, he was never a suspect to begin with. I just hope I can sell Chief Harper on that idea. It won't be easy. Harper's desperate for a lead."

"No kidding. It looks bad on your record when the police station's broken into. Makes for an uncomfortable TV interview."

"Oh. That reminds me. We are *not* telling Rick Reed."

"How come?"

"I promised the chief I wouldn't. After all, *he* doesn't think I'm guilty."

"Sergeant Crowley does?"

"I wouldn't think so, under the circumstances. Of course, men can justify just about anything when sex is involved."

"Oh," Becky said. "Tough talker. I think you really like the guy."

Cora shrugged. "I liked all of them in the beginning." She waggled her hand. "Except maybe Melvin."

Cora was unhappy driving home. For a lot of reasons. In the first place, she was driving home. Instead of spending the night at Sergeant Crowley's. Which any girl old enough to have flown the nest would be doing. At least Cora would. Good men didn't come along that often. Hell, at her age, *mediocre* men didn't come along that often.

Not that she was old. Cora subscribed to the idea you're only as old as you feel. She also subscribed to the idea that having to say that meant you were old.

The real reason she was upset was that she told Becky Baldwin about Sergeant Crowley. She didn't have to do that. Becky didn't have a boyfriend. It was like rubbing her nose in it. Cora knew why she'd done it, trying to bounce back after Barney Nathan. Letting people *know* she'd bounced back after Barney Nathan was somehow important to her. And the number of people she could tell was limited. Sherry wouldn't understand. Well, she would, but she wouldn't approve. It would also make her nervous—anything involving the police did. Though, Cora realized, that wasn't really fair. Sherry had a child to raise, and protect, and obsess about. A little girl to shield from her crazy aunt's exploits. Sherry'd be projecting it on her. Imagining her sweet little girl being led astray by the wicked policeman.

Cora drove in the driveway. The addition was dark, with the exception of a flickering light, most likely from the television, in Sherry and Aaron's window. They were in bed, just as Cora would have been if the police station hadn't been broken into. Or if she didn't have a damn curfew. If it weren't for that, she'd not only be in bed, she'd be in a different bed entirely and life would be good. Chief Harper wouldn't have found her. Even if he'd called Crowley, the sergeant wouldn't have admitted she was there. She'd have gotten the news about the break-in without having to do anything about it. And she'd cuddle with her man, and all would be right with the world.

Life wasn't fair.

Cora got out of the car and slammed the door. Regretted it immediately. No reason to wake Sherry and Aaron if they'd fallen asleep in front of the TV. That was one of the joys of having a TV in your bedroom, you could fall asleep watching a show. Cora wondered if she should put one in hers. After all, fair was fair. The sudoku books were doing well. Why the hell not? It would give her something to do in bed.

Cora grimaced at the thought. It kind of took the joy out of the whole idea.

Cora went in, locked the door, and switched off the living room lights. She considered detouring into the kitchen for a cup of coffee. Rejected the idea. There was none, and she'd have to make it. More trouble than it was worth.

Cora made her way down the hallway, guided by the light from the bedroom. Only it wasn't just from the bedroom. There was a light coming from the office as well.

Cora blinked. She hadn't turned on the light in the office. Why should she? And she hadn't gone to bed with it on. It would have kept her awake. Hell, even the faintest light from the kitchen kept her awake. She always had to get up and turn it off. Or close her bedroom door. And with Sherry and Aaron upstairs, she liked to leave it open. So by rights, the light should be off.

Cora looked in the door.

The computer was running. The screen saver was on, so she couldn't tell what program was open.

Cora frowned. There was no reason for Sherry to be using her computer. As far as Sherry knew, Cora was asleep. And Sherry had her own computer upstairs. Unless Aaron was using it. But he had no reason to; he had a laptop. And even if he *was* using it, what was so damn urgent Sherry couldn't wait?

Cora went over, clicked the mouse.

Roused from its sleep, the computer yawned, stretched, made waking-up noises. It flashed twice, once with a blank screen, once with a screen unknown outside of computer geek circles. With a whir, the program opened and the image on the screen was restored.

It was a crossword puzzle.

Across

1 EMT's skill
4 __ Jean, a.k.a. Marilyn
9 Pearly Gates saint
14 Place to graze
15 Sell online
16 Still in the running
17 Message from the killer
19 Calyx part
20 "Go ahead!"
21 Fresh-mouthed
22 Title for McCartney
23 Thither's partner
24 Sole serving
27 More of the message
33 Be gaga over
34 Reese's "Legally Blonde" role
35 Bring crashing down
36 Gradually slower, in mus.

(continued)

(continued)

37	Myna's skill
40	Blaster's need
41	Sighters of pink elephants
43	Campbell of "Scream" movies
44	Raring to go
46	Still more of the message
48	Cropped up
49	Newly minted naval off.
50	Telephonic trigram
51	Defeater of Tilden
54	Chips' spicy go-with
59	Deliver a keynote
60	End of the message
61	Suez Canal user
62	"__ the worst"
63	Mushy fare
64	Say "Nyah nyah" to
65	Juice, as a goose
66	Pronoun in rebuses

Down

1 Gridiron infraction
2 Ring out
3 10K, for one
4 Wire service delivery
5 Catchall column
6 Bug spray brand
7 O'Shea of "The Verdict"
8 Many a microbrew
9 Hand down
10 First Lady before Bess
11 Pool cue ends
12 NASA "walks"
13 Have trust
18 Perp subduer
23 River of Flanders
24 Language of Iran
25 "Talk turkey" is one
26 "Whole __ Love"
27 Gulf of Aden land
28 Mixologist's garnish
29 Worrier's risk, it's said
30 Expenditure
31 Fan mags
32 __ nous
38 Rustic stopovers
39 "Likely story"
42 Add inducements to
45 Sans-serif typeface
47 Magazine ad, sometimes
50 Be a bad winner
51 Holler's companion
52 Diva's delivery
53 China/Korea border river
54 Soft seat
55 Nautical assents
56 Get an illegal pre-race transfusion
57 Words to an old chap
58 Le Pew of cartoons
60 Bro, e.g.

Cora scowled.

Of course. Sherry had installed *Crossword Compiler* so she could work on Cora's computer on those odd times when hers wasn't available. Using it this time of night just because Cora had to run out seemed an abuse of privilege. In any event, leaving the program open and the lights on was inconsiderate. Since Cora couldn't use *Crossword Compiler,* it was almost a deliberate slap in the face.

Sherry would hear about this.

Cora was tempted to leave the puzzle on the screen to confront Sherry with, but she wanted to check her e-mail. And even though Sherry had shown her how to shrink the program to a tiny icon on the bottom of the screen, having it open made the computer slower. And it was slow enough already. Cora wondered if it was time to treat herself to a new one.

One without *Crossword Compiler.*

Still, Cora wanted to confront Sherry with the puzzle. Not tonight, but tomorrow.

Cora sat down, moved the mouse, clicked on FILE. A bunch of options opened. She moved the mouse again, clicked on PRINT. That brought up the PRINT PREVIEW screen, asking if she wanted to send the job to the laser jet printer, an unnecessary question since she had no other. It also offered her the chance to make multiple copies, also not relevant to her situation. It was rare Cora wanted to print even one copy of a puzzle, let alone several.

Cora left the settings unchanged, clicked the PRINT icon again.

The printer whirred and spit out the puzzle.

Cora picked it up, turned it over, verified that it was indeed the puzzle and not some recipe for shortcake that had been in the printing cue ahead of her own job, which for some reason had not printed. Which would not have surprised her in the least. But, no, it was the puzzle.

Cora closed *Crossword Compiler,* checked her e-mail. All spam. She wondered if Sergeant Crowley had e-mail. Maybe at the station. She hadn't seen a computer in his apartment. Of course, she hadn't been looking.

She shut down the computer, switched off the light, and took the crossword puzzle to her bedroom. She'd thrown her nightgown over the back of the chair. She didn't feel like sleeping in a night-gown. She felt like sleeping in panties and a shirt. Actually, she felt like sleeping in a *man's* shirt, but no matter. She changed into a baggy T-shirt and got in bed.

Alone. With no television. Oh, it was the wrong time for Sherry to have left *Crossword Compiler* open.

Cora picked up the crossword from her night table and looked at it with righteous indignation.

Her face froze.

Clue 17 Across was: Message from the killer.

Cora burst through the door.

Sherry and Aaron were snuggled in bed watching a TV show. Startled, Sherry sprang up to a sitting position. "Cora!"

"Oh, thank God!" Cora wheezed. She was huffing and puffing and trying to catch her breath after sprinting up the stairs.

"Are you crazy?" Sherry said. "What the hell do you think you're doing?" She spotted the paper in Cora's hand. "Is that a crossword puzzle?" she said accusingly.

Cora looked, realized she was still holding it. "Yeah," she gasped.

"Well, if you think I'm solving it now, you're dreaming."

Cora waved her hands. "No, no, no." She felt dizzy from hyperventilating and sank indecorously to the floor, her T-shirt pulled up to her waist.

"Cora!" Sherry sprang out of bed to help, noticed her attire. "You're not dressed."

"I'm wearing the same thing you are."

Sherry, who was indeed wearing a T-shirt and panties, looked at her aunt in exasperation. "I'm married."

"Nice, nice, throw it in my face," Cora muttered.

"Are you all right?" Aaron said. He was wearing boxer shorts and a T-shirt, his usual nighttime garb, but no one seemed to care.

Cora waved it away. "I'm fine, I'm fine. I just ran up the stairs. I was scared to death."

"Why?" Sherry said.

Cora's eyes widened. "Oh, no!"

She sprang up and ran out the door. Sherry and Aaron were right on her heels.

With a growing sense of dread, Cora lunged down the hall, flung open the door to the baby's room.

Jennifer was lying on her belly with her bottom in the air. She seemed fine, but Cora hurried over to the crib, peered closer. She couldn't tell a thing. The baby lay absolutely still.

Cora reached out her finger and poked her.

"Cora!" Sherry gasped.

Jennifer stirred, contracted, stretched, lay still again.

Sherry grabbed Cora's arm and dragged her toward the door. "What the hell are you doing?"

"The killer was in the house."

"*What?*"

Back in the bedroom, Cora gave Sherry and Aaron a rundown of the situation.

"The police station was broken into?" Aaron said.

"Right, right, *that's* the important thing," Sherry said.

"He's a newspaper reporter," Cora said. "Which reminds me, the chief doesn't want it given out."

"What?" Aaron said.

"Never mind the police station," Sherry said impatiently. "The killer was in the house? Where the hell was Buddy?"

"Unfortunately, he can be bought off with a couple of puppy treats."

"Who would know that?" Aaron said.

"Good point. I don't know the answer, but it's certainly a good question."

"I don't believe this," Sherry said. "While you were gone to the police station, the killer came in, used the computer, created a crossword puzzle?"

"I know," Cora said. "It boggles the mind. But it happened." She frowned. "Would he have time to do it? It's not like I was gone that long. I mean, sitting there, with the added pressure of not knowing when I was coming home. Could it be done?"

"I don't know. How long were you gone?"

"Under an hour. Could he do it in that time?"

"Not unless he had nerves of steel. But he didn't have to do it that way."

"What do you mean?"

"He could have constructed it in advance, on another computer. All he had to do was come in here with a memory stick, plug it into your computer, download the puzzle into *Crossword Compiler,* and call it up on the screen."

"Damn."

"What do you mean, 'damn'?"

"If it could be that easily done, it probably was."

"As opposed to what?" Sherry said. "It's *there.* I didn't put it there and you sure as hell didn't put it there, so *someone* put it there, no matter *how* hard it was."

Cora put up her hands. "I know, I know, that was a stupid thing to say. It's just the more plausible this is, the more it freaks me out. So, someone came in here just to put a crossword puzzle on the computer." Her eyes widened. "Do you suppose he broke into the police station to get me out of here so he could do it?"

"That's convoluted as all hell."

"What's your point?" Cora sighed. "Well, I guess we better call Chief Harper."

"I called Chief Harper," Aaron said.

"You did?"

"Damn right I did. Just as soon as you said the killer was in the house. He'll be right over."

"Oh, my God!" Cora said.

"What's wrong?"

"Sherry, you've gotta solve the crossword puzzle before he gets here. Otherwise, he'll want me to do it."

"Give it here," Sherry said. She snatched up a pencil and a magazine to write on, sat on the bed to work on the puzzle. She was still working when headlights came up the driveway.

"Hurry up!" Cora said.

"Thanks for the advice," Sherry muttered. "And . . . there!" She handed it to Cora. "Here. Better take a look so you're at least familiar with it."

Cora snatched it up and read the killer's message.

I act while
You snooze
I'm a winner
So you lose.

"What do you think it means?" Harper said.

"I have no idea what it means," Cora said. "Except the killer is taunting me. Which is not a new revelation."

They were all gathered in the living room in Cora's end of the house so as not to disturb Jennifer. Aaron had the baby monitor in his pocket. He had pulled on his trousers. Sherry was in her robe. Cora had slipped into her Wicked Witch of the West costume, the favorite old tattered frock she wore around the house.

"Yeah, but now he's getting more specific. Saying you can't win. Like this was a game."

"It's always been a game," Cora said. "That's the problem. We started out treating it seriously. Why is the town hall broken into? It amuses him. Why is the police station broken into? It amuses him."

"What's this about the police station being broken into?" Aaron said.

"Oh, for Christ's sake!"

"Hey, if the police station was broken into, you want me handling it in a serious article, or you want Rick Reed treating it as a joke?"

Harper took a breath. "The police station was broken into. We believe it has something to do with the break-in at town hall and the murder of the town clerk."

"What leads you to believe that?"

"As if she hasn't already told you."

"All I said was that's where I was while the killer was here planting the puzzle."

"You also speculated on whether the break-in at the police station was just to lure you out of the house," Aaron said.

"Is that what you think?" Harper said to Cora.

"It's possible, but I don't think so. I think he broke into the police station because he wanted to break into the police station."

"What makes you think that?" Aaron said.

"Hang on a minute here." Harper waggled a finger at Aaron. "You are not conducting an interview in my presence as if I gave it my tacit approval. Any views Cora expresses are entirely her own, and I don't want to be quoted on them."

"Unless they turn out to be right," Cora muttered.

Harper gave her a look.

"I would say this," Cora said. "And this is my opinion not the chief's and he may totally not agree with me. The killer may not have robbed the police station to get me out of my house, but he knew that would be the result. Because he came here and planted the crossword puzzle. And he wouldn't have had that in mind unless he thought it was a likely consequence of his action."

Aaron nodded. "That sounds good. You want to second that, Chief?"

"Keep me out of it."

"You're the chief of police."

"You wanna question me as the chief of police, fine. Don't ask me to be her cheerleader."

"That wasn't my intention."

Headlights flickered up the driveway.

"Someone's coming," Sherry said.

"Probably just Dan Finley," Aaron said.

Harper shook his head. "It better not be. I told him to hold down the station."

"Then who is it?" Sherry said. Her voice sounded strained.

Cora snatched up her purse from the coffee table and pulled out her gun.

"Cora!" Harper said.

"If it's Dan, I won't shoot him." Cora flung open the door.

A car pulled up and Sergeant Crowley got out.

"Son of a bitch!" Cora said. "What are you doing here?"

Crowley came striding up the path. "Are you kidding me? The killer was in your house." He pushed by Cora in the door. "Well, well, the gang's all here. You must be the niece. And you must be that reporter she married."

"I'm Sherry Carter. This is Aaron Grant."

"And this is my arresting officer," Cora said. She turned on Chief Harper accusingly. "What the hell is he doing here?"

"I called him. The killer broke into your house and I'm not going to call him?"

"You also tell him he broke into the police station?"

"What?" Crowley said.

"Let's not get sidetracked. The killer broke into the police station, possibly as a ruse to get her out of the house to plant the crossword puzzle on her computer."

Crowley turned to Cora. "What crossword puzzle?"

"Another slap in the face, telling me I'm too stupid to solve the crime."

"That's nothing new."

"Thanks a lot."

"Where's the puzzle?"

Cora scooped it up from the coffee table. "Here."

"You handled it?"

"It's a computer printout. The killer never touched it."

"But he printed it out?"

"*I* printed it out. On a blank piece of paper," Cora said impatiently.

If Crowley was impressed, he didn't show it. He looked at it, looked back at Cora. "*You* printed this out?"

"That's right."

"And it was on *your* computer?"

"Uh-huh."

"You expect me to believe someone came in here and created it on your computer while you were at the police station?"

"Hang on a minute," Chief Harper said. "Are you implying she could have done it herself?"

"Oh, don't be a horse's ass!" Cora said.

No one was surprised that she said it. They *were* surprised that she said it to *Chief Harper*. He took a step back, looked shocked.

Cora flushed, embarrassed at having automatically defended Crowley. "He doesn't suspect me of doing that any more than you do, Chief. He's just a New York cop, and that's how they talk."

Crowley put up his hands. "Please, don't let me give offense. Then she'll clam up and call in that lady lawyer and we won't get anywhere. So, you got two break-ins and a homicide. What makes you think it's my killer?"

"The crossword puzzle."

"Of course," Crowley said. He sighed. "You got any coffee?"

"I didn't know I was entertaining," Cora said. She curtsied. "You probably couldn't tell from my ball gown."

"I'll make some," Sherry said. "You got that baby monitor turned on?"

Aaron pulled it out of his pocket. They could hear the crackle from the microphone. Satisfied, Sherry went into the kitchen.

Crowley turned to Chief Harper. "The way I understand it, you got her here because you don't have the manpower to guard her and she's got a gun." Before the chief could retort, Crowley said, "Where the hell'd she get a gun, anyway? You give it to her?"

"It's my gun," Cora said impatiently. "You think I got only one gun? Then every time I got arrested for murder, I'd be unarmed."

Crowley's eyes never left the chief. "You knew she had a gun?"

Harper stuck out his chest. "She has every right to have a gun, Sergeant. Just because you arrested her doesn't mean she's guilty."

"Just because a pyromaniac hasn't been convicted of arson doesn't mean you give him matches."

"Boys, boys," Cora said. "A little less macho posturing would be nice. How about we concentrate on catching this killer?"

"Unless you think you already have her," Harper said.

Crowley wasn't backing down on any point. "I'm not ruling it out."

"Of course not. You wanna tell me why? Can you come up with any reason whatsoever? She has no conceivable motive. She'd have to be insane."

"And that's a deal breaker?"

"Hey!" Cora said. "I'm right here."

"The point is," Crowley said, "suspect or not, she's in danger. You believe it. I believe it." He turned to Cora. "You got a spare bedroom?"

Cora did her best to keep her voice neutral. She gestured to Sherry, who had just come in from the kitchen with a tray of coffee. "There's Sherry and Aaron's room. They moved upstairs."

"Fine. I don't feel like driving back to the city anyway. Let's sit down, have some coffee, see if we can make some sense out of this mess."

"Crowley slept over."

Becky looked up from her desk. "Huh?"

Cora flopped down in the client's chair and pulled a pack of cigarettes out of her purse. "He and Chief Harper had a fight over me. It was very flattering."

Cora lit a cigarette. Becky was too astonished to protest.

"The killer was in your house?"

"The killer was in my house. No big deal. I wasn't there. The killer knew I wouldn't be there. He just wanted to leave a cross-word puzzle on my computer."

"Not knowing you couldn't solve it."

"I have no idea what this killer knows and doesn't know."

"You coming back to Dennis?"

Cora waved her hand impatiently. "No. Don't get me wrong. I don't know who it is. I know who it *isn't*."

"So, Crowley stayed over. Does Sherry know?"

"She made him coffee."

"In the morning?"

"No. Last night. When the boys were fighting over me."

Becky rubbed her forehead. "Please. I had one too many drinks at the Country Kitchen. You wanna fill me in?"

Cora described the events at her house.

"So. Sergeant Crowley stayed in Sherry and Aaron's room?"

"Well, I had him mess up the sheets so it looks like he did."

"Cora."

"Relax. We're both grown-ups and we both have guns. We're perfectly safe."

"And we're no closer to solving this crime."

"In a way we are."

"What way would that be?"

"Killer's getting bolder. Breaks into the police station as soon as Dan Finley leaves. Breaks into my house as soon as I leave. With Sherry and Aaron there. And with Buddy there. All he had to do was bark and alert them. And he didn't."

"Isn't there a story like that? The dog that didn't bark?"

"Yup. Sherlock Holmes. I'm not sure if Buddy's read it."

"Seriously."

"In Buddy's case, he'll shut up if you throw a puppy biscuit on the floor. That's all the killer had to do. He just had to know to do it."

Becky considered that. "You think it's someone local?"

"Why not?"

"Because of the New York angle."

"Well, it's someone local to somewhere. It could be here, it could be New York. It could be both."

"How could it be both?"

"A lot of people have country houses. Or move. I did. I'm local to here and New York. New York is my old stomping ground. I still consider myself a New Yorker."

"Yeah, but he must not live in Bakerhaven."

"Why do you say that?"

"He broke into town hall. A local wouldn't have to do that. He could walk right in."

"Not if he wanted something they wouldn't give out."

"Like what?"

"I have no idea. If I did, we'd know what it was."

"There must be some way to find out."

"How? The only person who'd know is dead."

"And that's undoubtedly why she is. So, what did the town clerk know that the killer didn't? And why would finding it out seal her doom?"

"'Seal her doom'? Boy, that's melodramatic."

"You prefer 'cause her to be killed'?"

"I don't prefer anything."

Becky got up and went into the little bathroom half-hidden behind her file cabinet. She emerged a minute later with a bottle of Advil and a glass of water. She shook three pills out into her hand.

"Isn't that more than you need?"

"Right. Like I'm going to OD on ibuprofen."

"It's a bad habit to get into."

"Oh, yeah? You remember when you used to drink?"

"Not very much."

"Then let me take my pills." Becky popped the pills in her mouth and washed them down with a sip of water. "There. The effects should be instantaneous. They're not, but they should be."

"I'm glad you're getting your sense of humor back."

"I'm not getting anything back. I'm trying to forestall your comments by making my own. At least I don't get a headache trying to follow them."

"Are you this open with all your clients, or do you usually pretend you're vaguely coherent?"

"Most clients wouldn't get to see me until I choose to see them. You're the only one comes crashing through the door expecting me to spring into action."

"Would you be less antagonistic if I weren't sleeping with Crowley?"

"Will you stop saying that? I have enough trouble defending you without having to prove you're not a promiscuous lush."

"I stopped drinking years ago."

"I rest my case."

"What?"

"Only people with drinking problems do that."

"Good point. Wanna go get a drink?"

"What?"

"When I was drinking, the only real cure for a hangover was a good, stiff drink."

"I'll keep it in mind."

Cora left Becky's and went over to the police station. Dan Finley was on the phone when she came in. He covered the mouthpiece. "Chief's at Town Hall."

Cora nodded and went over to the town hall building.

She figured Dan meant the county clerk's office. She figured right. The chief was there. So was Sergeant Crowley. The chief was standing around looking glum. Crowley was going over the files.

"What's he doing here?" Cora said.

Harper grunted. "Better ask him."

Crowley looked up from the file cabinet. "I'm not having any luck with my crime, so I'm trying to solve yours. Chief thinks I'm stepping on his toes, but I'm not."

"That may well be," Cora said. "But I imagine he takes it as a comment on his job."

"Yeah, well, it isn't. It's a comment on mine. I'm getting nowhere. Zip, zero, zilch. What makes it worse, I got six detectives on the case, and we still can't come up with anything. I'm at a dead end. I'm desperate." He turned to Harper. "You *don't* have six detectives combing through every bit of evidence. So I got a shot at finding something new. Plus, your break-in happened before my murder. The guy may not have had everything worked out yet. He may have been careless. He may have made a mistake."

"Yes, isn't that diplomatic," Harper said. "You know what it looks like? You stay over because you don't trust me to protect her. You review the evidence because you think I missed something. Bottom line is you don't think I can do my job."

"I'm sorry you feel that way."

"What are you doing?" Cora said.

Crowley had taken a drawer out of the file cabinet and set it on the floor. He sat down next to it and pawed through the files. "I'm trying to figure out what there could be in there that would be of interest to someone who wanted to kill somebody in New York."

"That's stupid," Cora said.

"Thanks a lot." Crowley looked up at Harper. "Is she usually this supportive?"

"That's nothing. Wait'll you hit her with a theory."

"*Why* is that stupid?" Crowley said.

"New York is incidental. *I'm* the Bakerhaven connection."

"First thing I looked for. And I can't find a thing."

Cora looked at the file cabinet. "You looked in here for me?"

"Yes."

"Under Cora Felton?"

"Yes, of course."

"Well, there's your problem. I wasn't Cora Felton when I came here. I was Cora Crabtree."

"What?"

"Legally," Cora said. She waggled her hand. "Well, semi-legally. Melvin Crabtree is my ex-husband. When I moved here I was still using his name. We were divorced, but he was paying me alimony. Still is, by the way. Anyway, I'm on the books as Cora Crabtree."

"Why, if you were divorced?"

"Because Sherry was hiding out from her ex-husband, and we didn't want any records anyone could look up. So I used my married name."

"Who would know that?"

"The town clerk," Harper said.

"Right. But why would that get her killed?"

"Well," Harper said, "if the killer broke in looking for Cora Felton, couldn't find her, and came back and asked the town clerk why not, then she'd become a liability."

"Yeah, but if he got the information, why would he break in again?"

"He broke into the police station," Cora pointed out.

"Yeah, but not to steal your file."

"Hey, you're not the only cop to ever arrest me. Lots of cops make mistakes."

"Thanks for the vote of confidence," Harper said dryly.

"Well, was I guilty?" Cora said. "I'm not saying you didn't have grounds. I'm saying the charges were dismissed."

"What charges?" Crowley said.

"That's not important," Cora said.

"I'll be the judge of that. What charges?" When Harper hesitated, he said, "It's a matter of public record."

"Then why didn't you ask for it?"

"I didn't know it was relevant."

"It's *not* relevant," Cora said irritably.

"Then why are you trying so hard to suppress it?"

Cora made a face. "I was arrested for murder a few years back."

"Murder?"

"Yeah, but I didn't do *that* one," Cora said. "So how could it possibly be relevant?"

"Now you're just playing with me," Crowley said.

"You see what I have to put up with?" Harper said.

"It's a wonder you're still sane."

"Boys, boys, I'm glad you're having fun at my expense, but you're missing the point. We're getting far afield. Just when things seemed promising. The killer breaks in here, looks for my file, doesn't find it. Questions the clerk, learns my file is Crabtree. By rights he should break in again, but he doesn't. Instead he kills the town clerk. Why does he do that?"

"So the town clerk can't identify him," Harper said.

"Yes, yes," Cora said impatiently. "That's gotta be the motive. The killer breaks in, can't find what he's looking for. He asks the town clerk, kills the town clerk. Doesn't make use of the information. Therefore the premise is wrong. The killer doesn't go back to the town clerk for more information. The killer gets all the information he needs during the break-in. Now, how can that be?"

"Maybe he knew you were Crabtree *before* he broke in," Crowley said.

Cora made a face. Next thing she knew, they'd be pinning it on Melvin. "That doesn't make sense. If he knew that much about me, why would he *need* to see my file?"

"I don't know, but I mean to find out," Crowley said. He clambered to his feet, pulled open the file cabinet drawer marked c, took out a file. "Let's see. Connors? No. *C-R.* Closer to the end. Here we go. Let's see. Cranwell, no. Ah! Here we are. Crabtree, Cora." He examined the file. "Appears all right. So, who would know if anything's missing?" He nodded ironically in answer to his own question. "The town clerk."

His cell phone rang. He muttered an imprecation, jerked it out of his pocket, and flipped it open. "Crowley . . . What! . . . You're kidding. I'll be right there!"

He flipped the cell phone shut.

"What's the matter?" Cora said.

"My apartment's been robbed."

"I should have seen this coming," Cora said.

"Oh, really?" Crowley said. He swerved around an SUV, rocketed down the Merritt Parkway.

"The killer broke into my house. The killer broke into the police station. It's only logical he'd break into your apartment, too."

"Why is that logical? He had no reason to break into my apartment."

"He had no reason to break into my house."

"Yes, he did. He left the crossword puzzle."

"Yeah, but why did he have to break in? He could have sent it in the mail. He could have taped it to the door like he did the last time."

"He wanted to put it on your computer."

"Why? One way or another, it's the same damn puzzle."

"He's making a point."

"What point?"

"That he could do it."

"Why isn't he making the same point with you?"

"I don't know."

"Exactly. The problem is we're trying to outthink this guy, and he may not be thinking. He may be just acting on impulse."

Crowley made a face and told another motorist what he thought of his driving skills.

"Why don't you put the siren on?"

"I don't like to do that."

"Why not?"

"It would be abuse of power."

"And going ninety isn't?"

"Hey, you watch your ethics, I'll watch mine."

"What's that supposed to mean?"

"At least I'm not pretending to be a police officer."

"Oh, low blow. If I cared, I'd be insulted."

"That's what I figured," Crowley said. "Anyway, I'm speeding to catch a murderer."

"He's long gone."

"Then I'm not going fast enough." Crowley weaved in and out of a couple of cars dawdling in the passing lane. It occurred to Cora the cars were probably dawdling at around seventy, and were darn glad the police car wasn't after them.

Crowley went down the West Side Highway as if it were the Indianapolis Speedway, cut off three lanes of heavy uptown traffic swerving onto West Twelfth Street, and flung the car through a series of frequent turns that sent pedestrians diving for cover.

Two cops were standing on the curb in front of his apartment. Crowley managed to miss them. He left Cora in the car and got out.

"All right, Officers, what have we got?"

The fatter cop was chewing gum. "We responded to a report of a burglary at this address. Found signs of a break-in, but no evidence that anything had been stolen."

"What signs of a break-in?"

"Front door had been pried with a crowbar, large screwdriver, or the claws of a hammer."

"You found it broken open?"

"We found it locked."

"How'd you get in?"

"Super let us in with a key. Apartment had not been ransacked, there were no obvious signs it had been searched. There was no way to tell if anything had been taken. We phoned it in, were instructed to wait here for you."

"You knew it was my apartment?"

"Not when we went in. All we had was the apartment number." He jerked his thumb at the other cop. "Officer Blake found your name on a piece of mail. We got out and called in."

"You're sure the perpetrator isn't still in the apartment?"

The cop looked pained by the question. "First thing we do, we secure the premises. Trust me, no one's there."

Crowley nodded. "Thanks, Officers. You can go."

"We have to file a report."

"Go ahead and file one."

"We have to verify if anything's missing."

"You said nothing was."

"We have to check with the owner."

Crowley smiled. "Officer, we're dealing with a guy who likes to get inside people's heads. He's more apt to leave something than take it. If he had, I think you'd've have found it, but by all means, let's take a look."

Crowley got Cora out of the car. "Miss Felton, right this way. Officers, this is one of the victims. Her house was broken into. If it's the same guy, she should know."

Upstairs, Crowley examined the damage to the door.

"Well, I can see where it's been pried, all right, but the hardware's all in place. If he got the door open, I don't know how he got it back in such good shape." Crowley whipped out his keys, turned one on the door. "Lock seems okay. Dead bolt's in place. Was it locked like this when you got here?"

"That's right."

"A full twist? The super didn't just give the key a quarter turn and it clicks open? A full three-sixty, moving the dead bolt, then the extra quarter?"

"Absolutely. I watched him do it. He stuck the key in the lock, turned it a full three-sixty degrees plus the quarter. Lock clicked open."

"Right you are." Crowley pushed the door open and strode in.

Cora hadn't realized what an anachronism the apartment was before, but with the eyes of the officers on it she did now. The Jimi Hendrix poster, for instance. Did these guys even know who Jimi Hendrix was?

"Okay," Crowley said. "I'm not searching my apartment, but I can tell you right off the bat nothing's missing. It's not the guy's MO. And if he left me something, he'd want it to be found. Go ahead and file your report. If two days from now I notice my hundred-thousand-dollar cuff links are missing, I'll be sure to let you know."

The officers nodded and left. When they were gone, Cora said, "You sure nothing's missing?"

"No."

"Wanna search the place?"

"Not particularly."

"What do you want to do?"

Crowley smiled. "Oh, we'll think of something."

Cora nuzzled her head against Crowley's chest. "You know," she murmured, we're not any closer to solving this."

Crowley shrugged. "Who cares?"

"That's the nicest thing you ever said to me."

"Even when I let you go?"

"That was pretty nice. But I think you did it more for shock value. You have a bit of a theatrical flair."

"Please. You'll get me drummed off the force."

"You prefer the dumb-cop image?"

"It's less trouble."

"How'd a guy like you get to be a cop, anyway?"

"John Jay College of Criminal Justice."

"Come on. You know what I mean."

"That's your hippie mentality talking. You grew up thinking cops are pigs and wonder why anyone could want to be one."

"This from a guy with a Jimi Hendrix poster on the wall."

"Again with stereotypes and labels. I happen to like his music."
Crowley scrunched up in bed. "Mind if I get a beer?"

"Mind if I smoke?"

"Disgusting habit."

"And drinking isn't?"

"You used to drink."

"I forgot. You read my file."

"We're not exactly strangers."

"That subject never came up."

"Not even at dinner?"

"The burger joint you took me to didn't have a wine list."

"I thought you liked burger joints."

"I do."

"Then what are we arguing about?"

"I don't know," Cora said. "It's too idyllic. Maybe I want to spoil it."

"Why?"

"Before it gets spoiled." Cora smiled. "Sorry. A shrink would have a field day with me. I had a groom get killed on me. I'm a little gun-shy."

"Sorry. I forgot."

"That's right. You know that, too." Cora changed the subject. "Did you mean what you said to those cops?"

"What?"

"You don't think the killer left anything."

"That's right."

"What makes you so sure?"

"In the first place, I don't think he got in. If he had, he'd want me to know it. He'd leave something to let me know what a bright boy he was, that locks can't stop him."

"Like what?"

"I don't know. But it would be obvious. Unless he planted a bug. You know, some sort of surveillance equipment."

"Oh, I don't think so," Cora said. Still, she couldn't help stealing a glance at the light fixture over the bed.

"You're pretty calm about this," Crowley said.

"I don't think we're in any danger."

"Why not?"

"If this guy wanted to hurt me, he'd hurt me. It's not like he hasn't had the chance. He followed me back to Bakerhaven. As far as he knew, I was a sitting duck. If he wanted me dead, I'd be dead. He doesn't want me dead. He wants to play with me."

"So do I," Crowley said.

Cora giggled. "Hang on, big boy. We're solving a crime here."

The phone rang.

Crowley rolled over and picked it up. He rolled back, said, "Hello? . . . Oh. Hi . . . *What?*"

Crowley sat straight up in bed, dumping Cora off him. "Broke in how? . . . Did you call the cops? . . . Yes, I know you called me. I mean the cops. . . . What do you mean, it's for me? . . . You're kidding! . . . Hang on, I'll be right there."

"Who was that?" Cora said.

Crowley looked at her, heaved a sigh. "My wife."

Chapter

3 9

Becky found Cora at a table in the back drinking a grande latte.

"What are we doing in Starbucks?" Becky said.

"Drinking coffee."

"Why couldn't we meet in the Country Kitchen?"

"I didn't want to be in a bar."

"Why not?"

"If I was in a bar, I might drink."

"Why?"

"He's married."

Becky's eyes widened. She sank down at the table. "Crowley's married?"

"Go ahead. Say I told you so."

"I didn't say anything."

"You thought it."

"You're a complicated person."

"Why don't you get a coffee."

"Do they have Irish coffee?"

"You can probably get it without the whiskey."

"What's Irish about that?"

Becky got a latte, came back, and sat down. She took a sip, grimaced, probably because it wasn't scotch.

"So he's married."

"Well, he's separated, but they're still legally married."

"Is it an amicable separation?"

"Not anymore."

"You mean she caught you with him?"

"Not exactly."

Cora told Becky about the phone call.

"He broke into Crowley's wife's house?"

"Since they're not divorced, technically the house is still his."

"He thought Crowley lived there?"

"No, he broke into his apartment, too. A least he tried to. When he couldn't get in, he had to improvise."

"Why'd he break into the house?"

"I don't know. I'm not on a first name basis with Mrs. Crowley, so I didn't go along to find out. I came back here to drown my sorrows in a cappuccino."

"If they're really separated, it's just the same as if they're divorced."

"Oh, yeah? Clearly you're not a divorce lawyer. If I'd known your views on the subject, I wouldn't have let you handle my alimony hearing against Melvin."

"You know what I mean. They've moved on. It's not like they have feelings for each other."

"If that were true, he wouldn't have jumped at the chance when I said I wouldn't go."

"Oh, really? Can you think of *any* ex-husband who'd like to bring his current girlfriend along to meet his ex-wife?"

"Sure. Melvin. He loved to rub your nose in it."

"All I'm saying is, you don't have to go from elation to despair in the blink of an eye. It's a surprise, it's not a disaster."

"Hey, trust me, sweetie. When you've been married as many times as I have, you know a disaster when you see one."

Becky's cell phone rang. She pulled it out, flipped it open. "Hello? . . . Yeah, this is Becky Baldwin. . . . Yeah, she's here." Becky covered the phone. "It's the disaster."

"I'm not here."

"I said you were."

"I don't want to talk to him."

Becky uncovered the phone. "She's playing hard to get."

Cora scowled. "Give me that." She snatched the phone out of her hand. "Crowley? Why are you calling my lawyer?"

"Well, you don't have a cell phone."

"I'm surprised you remembered."

"Why?"

"You're very forgetful. How's your wife?"

"Cora."

"I'm sorry I couldn't meet her, but I didn't want to cramp your style."

"Susan's freaked out. A killer broke into her house."

"Yeah. A killer broke into mine. Funny. We have something in common."

"In her case, it came out of the blue. She has no connection with me anymore, doesn't know what I'm doing, and had no idea I was being harassed by a killer."

"Among other things."

"Anyway, there's no doubt it's our guy, and no doubt he was in the house."

"Don't tell me."

"That's right. He left a crossword puzzle taped to the refrigerator. Has Becky got a fax?"

"Not in Starbucks."

"What are you doing in Starbucks?"

"You're a detective and you can't figure out what we're doing in Starbucks?"

"Okay, give me Becky's fax number and I'll send it to her office. I'll get it solved here, you get it solved there. See if you can figure out what it means. If there's any reason it was sent to the house."

"Oh, I'll be looking for that," Cora said. She passed the phone over to Becky. "Give him your fax number."

Becky, who'd heard only Cora's side of the conversation, said, "Why?"

"He wants to send you a Valentine. He fancies himself a lady killer."

Becky gave Crowley the number.

"Okay," Cora said. "Let's go over to your office and get the puzzle."

"What puzzle?"

Cora filled Becky in on their way to the office. The fax was already there. Becky pulled it out of the machine and handed it to Cora. "What do you think?"

Parnell Hall

Across

1 "Even __ speak ..."
5 Sailor's saint
9 Took a puddle-jumper, say
13 Molecule builder
14 Food bank freebie
15 Word in many parade names
16 Start of a message
18 Bucket-of-balls locale

19 Less forgiving
20 Not explicit
21 Dick was his running mate
22 __-Hawley Tariff Act
24 "__ la vista, baby"
27 More of the message
31 Sacrifice site
32 "All gone!"
33 Become tiresome
34 __ Canals

(continued)

(continued)

35 Dadaist Jean
37 Rye filler
39 Start of many German surnames
40 Lawsuit basis
42 Homecoming Weekend figure
44 Put one's two cents in
46 Still more of the message
48 MS. encls.
49 Like a new dollar
50 Where slop is served
51 Manti Te'o, ethnically
54 __ cushion (novelty store buy)
58 "Later, amigo!"
59 End of the message
61 Nemo's creator
62 Lone Star State sch.
63 Actress Soleil Moon __
64 Slaughter in Cooperstown
65 Recruit's fare
66 Ollie's pal

Down

1 Sounds of the awed
2 Bit of sabermetrics
3 Made a basket
4 Female retiree's title
5 Trebek or Sajak
6 Big name in small planes
7 Scratch up
8 Soccer stadium yell
9 Out of one's head
10 Innie clogger
11 Beat, barely
12 Dandelion, to many
15 Rap sheet item
17 Turkey's capital
20 Jimmy who mysteriously disappeared
22 __-Caps (candy brand)
23 "Good heavens!"
24 Must
25 Cool in manner
26 Rant and rave
27 Treats for bobbers
28 Graceland name
29 Nary a soul
30 Units of force
36 Busted, as a perp
38 Not quite all
41 Fat cats
43 Stereotypically blind official
45 Bribery outlays
47 Rub out
50 Bazaar units
51 Command under "File"
52 Mideast's Gulf of __
53 Surrealist Joan
54 Slingshot shapes
55 Fresh-mouthed
56 Irish New Ager
57 Genesis locale
59 Not talking
60 Absorbed, as a loss

Cora shrugged. "Looks like a crossword puzzle to me."

"Right. You have no idea. Want to take it to Harvey?"

"As long as we don't run into Chief Harper. He doesn't know I can't solve crosswords."

"You must have trouble keeping straight who knows what."

"You have no idea."

They took the puzzle over to Harvey Beerbaum's.

Cora didn't waste time on amenities. "Here, Harvey. Do your thing. It's all right. Becky knows I can't solve puzzles."

The portly cruciverbalist was somewhat taken aback. "Oh. Oh, I see. Would you like some tea?"

"No, Harvey. Just solve the damn puzzle before Chief Harper pops up and sees you doing it. He *doesn't* know I can't solve puzzles."

Harvey ushered them in and sat them at his dining room table. Cora could see the invisible pull being issued by the teakettle on the stove. He resisted manfully, sat down with the puzzle. "This was sent to you?"

"No. It was sent to Sergeant Crowley of the NYPD."

"Wasn't he the one who arrested you?"

"The very same," Cora said impatiently. "You wanna solve the puzzle?"

Harvey got to work.

Cora watched the pencil flying over the puzzle, frowned. "Your handwriting doesn't look anything like mine."

"What's that?" Harvey said without looking up. His pencil never stopped moving.

"If the chief saw it, it doesn't look like mine. Well, actually, it doesn't look like *Sherry's*. That's what the chief thinks is mine. So it wouldn't do any good for me to copy it over. And we don't have another unsolved puzzle for me to use, anyway."

Harvey never actually complained, but his nose crinkled slightly, and he managed to give the impression he was being buffeted by a swarm of bees. Nonetheless, he sped through the puzzle. "There," he said.

Cora snatched it out of his hand. At his expression, she said, "Sorry. I have a vested interest in this puzzle."

Cora read:

Have a care
Any friend
Of my enemy
May offend.

"Well, that's pretty clear. I'm the killer's enemy. If Crowley is my friend, *he's* the killer's enemy."

Harvey frowned. "Sergeant Crowley is your friend?"

Cora realized she'd misspoken. She didn't want to get into *that* with Harvey. "In a manner of speaking. We're both on the side of truth, justice, and the American way. Aside from the fact he arrested me. But that's a mistake anyone could make. Come on, Becky. We gotta tell the chief."

Cora herded Becky out to the car. "You taking this to the chief?"

"No, but we had to get out of there. You wanna discuss this in front of Harvey?"

"Not on your life. You gonna call Crowley?"

"Not right now. He's getting the puzzle solved at his end."

"He'd probably appreciate the heads-up."

"I would have appreciated it, too."

"You can't stay mad forever. This is a serious situation. We have a killer making threats."

"Veiled threats."

"That's the worst kind. You don't know what you're dealing with."

"Aw, hell," Cora said.

"What?"

"You're playing me again. That's how I know I've lost it. When I'm thinking irrationally, and you're making the deductions I usually make."

"So get a grip. This happened. What do you want to do?" At the look on Cora's face, Becky added quickly, "That would be helpful in terms of the legal aspects of the situation."

Cora took a breath, controlled herself. "I don't know what I want to do. The case just took a whole new direction. The killer had been taunting me by threatening the people close to me. Now the killer's threatening people close to Crowley."

"She's his ex-wife. She isn't close."

"The killer doesn't know that."

"And it wasn't necessarily for her. The house is in his name. The message could be for him."

Cora shook her head. "That doesn't fly. The killer broke into Crowley's apartment. He knows where he lives. He'd know that was a house where he *used* to live."

"If you say so."

"Well, what's wrong with that reasoning?"

"Nothing. But it's not a fact, it's a theory. There are other theories."

"Such as?"

"I have no idea. We're dealing with not enough information. Which appears to be how the killer likes it. Keeping us in the dark. Playing these little games. He's got to love the problems we're having."

"That's for sure," Cora said. "All right. It's Twisted Sister time."

"What?"

"We're not gonna take it. No more rolling over and playing dead. It's time to find out what's going on."

"How?"

"Well, not by asking Crowley. He's been a little too skimpy with the information. This time I wanna see for myself."

"Oh, yeah?"

"And I know exactly where to start."

Chapter

4 0

Mrs. Crowley lived in a small, two-story frame house with barely enough room for a driveway, but she had no reason to be jealous of her neighbors, none of whom had more land, and most of whom lived in even more modest structures. The house was still in Crowley's name, so Cora and Becky had no problem looking up the address. They went up the path, rang the bell.

The woman was dumpy. That was the first thing Cora noticed. She tried to see the attractive woman behind the plump exterior and failed. Crowley's ex-wife was an ordinary-looking middle-age woman with the sex appeal of a slug. Cora wondered what had ever attracted him to her. Of course, Crowley himself was no movie star. But the woman presented as a drab housewife, out of her depth and totally confused by the current goings-on.

"I don't understand," she said.

It was not the first time she'd said it. There were a lot of things that Crowley's ex-wife, whose name was Susan, didn't understand.

Cora trod gently, not wanting to turn the woman off and have her close down. "As I understand it, someone broke into your house and left a crossword puzzle on your refrigerator."

"Yes. It was frightening."

"As I said, I'm the Puzzle Lady. I have a reputation for dealing in crossword puzzles."

"Did you solve it?"

It was one of those questions Cora always tried to avoid. Though quite prepared to lie, when it came to crosswords, Cora always preferred to skirt the boundaries of the truth to create a false impression without ever actually saying something that wasn't so. Usually, she found, a simple deflection worked.

"I have it here," she said. "Would you like to see it?"

Susan reached out her hand eagerly. "Oh, yes. I'm very curious." She took the puzzle, looked it over. Her brow furrowed. "What's it mean?"

"You see the theme answer?"

"Theme answer?"

"The long answers. To the clues that say 'Start of message' and stuff like that."

Susan found them, read them off.

"I don't understand."

"Join the club."

"No. I don't understand any of this. Not just the crossword puzzle. I mean everything that's going on." She paused, then blurted. "He said you'd been arrested."

Cora looked at the woman and smiled. Of course. That was how Crowley would introduce her. A murder suspect who had something to do with crossword puzzles. Providing a reason for the crossword puzzle in the house. Well, not really a reason, just an association. An attempt to ground the whole thing in some semblance of reality. As bizarre as that reality might be. And to cast her in any role other than that of lover.

Cora nodded. "That is originally how I got involved in the case. A devious and resourceful man was attempting to link me to crimes with crossword puzzles. This young woman, Becky Baldwin, is my attorney, who kept me out of jail and will eventually clear me of the charge. In the meantime, the police have realized their mistake. Witness the fact they now share the evidence with me, hoping I can interpret it."

Becky smiled. "I'm sure they would drop the charges if they could, but it is now in the hands of the district attorney's office. Meanwhile, we're doing everything we can to solve this crime before it comes to court."

"But what's this about friends?"

"Some of the clues were sent directly to the sergeant. Some of the crossword puzzles seem to refer to him. This would be one of them. Particularly since it was attached to your refrigerator door."

Cora could see the woman's mind going, trying to follow all that. "And the friend he's talking about would be a friend of my husband's?"

Susan said *husband*, not *ex-husband*. Cora shot Becky a glance, but made no comment.

"That's right," Cora said. "There's no reason to be upset. Despite the fact the puzzle was found here. The house is still in your husband's name, isn't it?"

"Oh, yes."

"So a person looking it up could think he lived here."

"I suppose."

"And you're not his friend, you're his wife. At least his ex-wife."

"Oh, we're still married. But that's just a matter of convenience. Health insurance. Taxes. Things like that. He pays alimony, but it's not really alimony, because we're not divorced. It's a voluntary payment, per agreement. I must say, whatever other problems that man might have, he was a good provider. Never missed a payment."

"That's encouraging," Cora said. "Does he pay you in person?"

She smiled. "No, of course not. It's an automatic payment, directly into my checking account."

"Of course," Cora said. It seemed typical of Crowley's strange allure for women, that he would get credit for not missing an automatic payment. "So how often do you actually see him?"

"Before now? Oh, my goodness, it must be years. I can't even remember the last time I saw him."

Cora was feeling considerably better. Maybe Crowley wasn't such a cad after all. Maybe she should let him off the hook.

"So," Cora said. "When whoever left this puzzle talks about the friend of my enemy being no friend, it's very unlikely he'd be talking about you."

"Oh, I quite agree," Susan said. "It doesn't sound like me at all. I'm not a friend, I'm his wife. That sounds awful, but you know what I mean."

"Yes, of course."

Susan nodded in agreement with herself. "No, that sounds more like Stephanie."

"Stephanie?" Cora frowned. "Who's Stephanie?"

"His girlfriend."

Chapter

4 1

"Anything else you forgot to mention?"

Crowley looked up from his desk to find Cora looming over him. "I beg your pardon?"

"You have a wife *and* a girlfriend."

"Oh, hell."

"Is that all you have to say?"

Crowley glanced out the open door of his office. Cora was talking rather loud. "Could we discuss this somewhere else?"

"Where? In your bed? Not likely!"

"Could you keep your voice down?"

"Oh, I certainly wouldn't want to do anything to upset you."

"What brought this on?"

"You didn't mention you had a girlfriend."

"Who told you I had a girlfriend?"

"Your wife."

Crowley frowned. "You spoke to my wife?"

"Don't worry, I didn't give away any of your secrets. *She* did, though. It seems this girl Stephanie's played a major part in your life."

"You asked my wife about other women?"

"She only mentioned Stephanie. You mean there's more than one?"

Crowley looked like a man drowning. "You called on my wife and asked her about my love life?"

"Of course not. She volunteered the information. It seems to have been on her mind."

"Why did you go there at all?"

"I wanted to compare notes." At Crowley's reaction, she added, "About the break-in. Isn't that why you went to see her?"

"I sent you the crossword puzzle."

"Yeah. It says friends of mine are in trouble. If I had any, I'd warn them to watch it."

"Oh, for goodness' sakes," Crowley said. "You want to calm down, I'll tell you about Stephanie."

"I can't wait."

"Stephanie's an old friend. I've known her since high school. We used to date. After graduation we drifted apart. Got together a few years later. Broke it off again. When I got separated from Susan, we got together again. It didn't last."

"That's not the way your wife tells it."

Crowley sighed. "I'm sure it isn't. In Susan's version, Stephanie has claws and breathes fire."

"I was referring to the timeline more than the physical description. According to your wife, Stephanie showed up *before* you got separated. It was, in fact, one of the *causes* of the separation."

"Naturally there would be resentment."

"I'm glad you think it's natural," Cora said.

"What *isn't* natural is blaming me for something that didn't happen."

"What didn't happen?"

"Whatever it is you think did." Crowley took a breath. "Look,

I have other cases besides yours. A double homicide just came in. I can't ignore it just because my ex-wife mentioned my ex-girlfriend. Where did you see her, by the way?"

"In her house. Or *your* house, if I understand correctly."

"Were you this antagonistic with her?"

"I took Becky along to make sure I behaved myself. She only had to wrestle me to the ground once."

"Did you find anything I'd overlooked?"

"Is that the same as 'neglected to mention'?"

"Aside from the puzzle on the refrigerator. Did you find any evidence?"

"No."

"Can this keep till tonight?"

"Sure, but we won't be discussing it then."

"Why not?"

"Because you'll be in the city. Your bodyguard duties are over. We Bakerhaven people can do quite well on our own."

"I understand you're upset, but this is serious. We're dealing with a killer."

"I'll be fine. I'm armed, and Bakerhaven's finest are ever vigilant."

"Bakerhaven's finest consist of one officer doing a drive-by once or twice a night."

"There's an advantage to that."

"What?"

"They don't sleep over."

"All right. Stay here. I'll put you in a hotel with an armed guard at the door."

"And will you come tiptoeing in on little cat feet to try to talk some sense into me?"

"I won't go near the place. I'll be busy catching up on all the work that's gone to hell while I was out of town."

"So now I've wrecked your career."

"You've certainly put a damper on my day. Aside from everything else, I've gotta worry about you getting killed."

"I'm sorry if that's a distraction."

"Look. Stay in town. Meet me after work. We'll talk this over."

Cora chuckled. "Yeah, sure. That reminds me of something I used to tell Melvin toward the end of the marriage."

"What's that?"

"Not tonight, dear, I've got a headache."

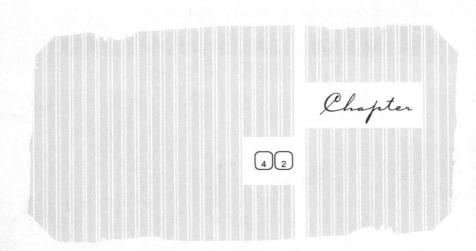

Chapter

4 2

Jennifer spun in a circle, fell to the floor, and giggled hysterically.

The audience, consisting of Cora, Sherry, and Aaron, laughed and applauded.

"For an encore she does pratfalls," Aaron said.

"That wasn't a pratfall?" Cora said.

"Not at all," Sherry said. "That was a perfectly choreographed ballet move."

"You're grooming her to be a ballerina?"

"She can be whatever she wants," Sherry said.

"As long as she stays away from teenage boys," Aaron added.

"Teenage boys? She isn't even two."

"Hey, it's our little girl. You gotta start teaching 'em young."

"And by the time they're sixteen, they're smoking dope and have a nose ring and tattoos."

"Don't give her any ideas," Sherry said.

"Right," Cora said. "Her eyes lit up just at the mention."

"So, when's that cop showing up?" Aaron said.

"He's not."

"Really? How come?"

Cora shrugged. "Guess we're just not that important anymore. Killer's turned his attention to the city. Broke into Crowley's apartment and the house of his ex-wife. That's undoubtedly who they're protecting."

"Do you think they're in any danger?" Sherry said.

"How should I know? We're dealing with a lunatic who doesn't seem to have much sense of purpose. Just gets off on terrorizing people. There's no telling why he's doing what he's doing, he's just doing it. Anyway, he seems to have moved on."

"So no one's guarding the house?"

"I'm guarding the house. Unless you want Dan Finley to hang out all night. I assure you, I'll do a much better job."

A sharp sound made Cora jump. But it was not the killer breaking in. It was Jennifer knocking an ornate paperweight off an end table. She immediately burst into tears.

Sherry leapt up. "Oh, my God, is she all right?"

"She's just scared," Aaron said.

"It fell on her foot."

"It never touched her."

"I knew we should get rid of that paperweight."

Cora smiled. If Sherry knew that, she had never voiced her opinion.

Sherry whisked Jennifer away from the scene of the trauma, carried her back to her end.

Aaron shook his head. "Jennifer coddling."

"What?" Cora said.

"That's like mollycoddling, only with Jennifer."

"Aaron. Take a tip from me. That's one of those remarks that is amusing only to people who are not your wife."

"I know," Aaron said. "Sherry's just upset. About the cop not being here. Not that she thought we needed him. She thought it was stupid. But you take him away, it's like cutting a lifeline."

"I understand," Cora said. "But in terms of a bodyguard, I'm not sure that cop was very effective. The guy was snoring before my head ever hit the pillow."

Aaron followed Sherry out to the addition, leaving Cora alone with her thoughts. Which wasn't good. She was still in a state of mind where being in a bar might be dangerous. Just being alone in the *house* might have been dangerous, had there been any source of temptation, but there had been no liquor on the premises ever since Cora got sober. Sherry might have some cooking wine, but Cora wasn't tempted to look for it. That was the sort of thing she'd do only once she'd begun drinking and run out of booze. It was never a place to start.

Always a first time.

The phrase ran though Cora's mind, had a chilling effect.

Cora glanced around.

Why the hell was she in the kitchen? Her feet led her there. Not powered by any conscious thought. Just wandering aimlessly. So why was she there?

Ah. Hot cocoa. That's the ticket. That would be comforting. A good way to fall asleep. Get in bed with a nice cup of hot chocolate.

Cora frowned. How did you make hot chocolate, anyway? Sherry'd always made it. How did she do it? With milk? With water? Definitely with chocolate. What kind of chocolate? Not chocolate syrup. Powdered chocolate. That's right. A tin of powdered chocolate. You pried the top off with a spoon. Let's see. That would be in a cupboard, wouldn't it?

Cora opened the cupboard. Encountered a myriad of spices and condiments. None large enough to be a tin of chocolate.

Cora closed the cupboard door. Turned to the other wall. Three cupboard doors beckoned to her. Too many choices. Way too hard. She didn't want cocoa anyway.

Cora slumped down at the kitchen table. Her eyes misted over. She put her head in her hands.

"Cora?" Sherry stood in the doorway. She looked concerned. "What's wrong?"

Cora waved her hand. "I was going to make cocoa, but I forgot how to do it."

"You didn't forget. You never do it. You want cocoa, I'll make some."

"You don't have to do that."

"Aaron's got Jennifer. I snuck out."

Sherry pulled open the middle cupboard door, took out a can of Nesquik. She popped the top. "Here, I'll join you. Girls' night out."

Sherry put heaping spoonfuls into two cups, added water, stirred it around, filled the cups with milk.

"Oh. Water *and* milk," Cora said.

Sherry popped one cup in the microwave, zapped it forty-five seconds on high. "I don't know about this. Hot cocoa's going to put you to sleep. What with you being the bodyguard, and all."

Cora said nothing.

Sherry looked at her. "What's wrong?"

The microwave beeped. Sherry took out the coffee cup, tested it with her finger, slid it in front of Cora, and zapped her own.

"Come on, Cora, what's up?"

"Brenda's pregnant."

Sherry's eyes widened. "What?"

Cora couldn't meet her eyes. "You got me worried about Dennis, talking about who might have a grudge against you. You know it's nothing, I know it's nothing. I still checked it out."

"Brenda's pregnant?"

"Yeah. You didn't hear it from me. She wanted to be the one to tell you. I said I wouldn't say anything."

"Cora, that's not good."

"I know, I know. Of course that's how you feel."

"What's she going to do?"

"She's going to have a baby. It's not the end of the world. Other women have done it."

"But—"

"It's okay. I went there to check Dennis out. Guess what? He passed. I don't know what happened, but the fact is, he's moved on. He's not thinking about your family, he's thinking about his. It doesn't mean I won't keep tabs on him, and at the slightest sign of trouble I'll violate his parole. But there's every indication this is a good thing."

"I wish I could believe that."

"I know. You get bad news so often, you can't believe good news when it comes. Look. Take your cocoa, go back to bed. Tell Aaron you're upset because Brenda's pregnant. He'll think of something absurdly comforting to say."

"Like what?"

"It doesn't matter, just as long as he's saying it. You'll obsess about it and you'll go to sleep. You'll call Brenda tomorrow and let her tell you. She'll say Dennis is changed. You won't be impressed, because you've heard it before, but something will be different and you'll pick up on it because you're very good."

Cora took her hot chocolate into her room, got in bed. Despite the warm liquid, she did not feel tired. If anything, she was more keyed up than ever.

Brenda's pregnant. She hadn't meant to tell Sherry that. She meant to let Brenda tell her. But Sherry'd seen she was upset, and she had to say something. She didn't want to talk about Crowley, didn't want to bring it up. She brought up Dennis instead. Selfishly. Making Sherry upset rather than upset herself. Had she really done that?

Cora sipped the cocoa. It wasn't making her drowsy. She wondered if she should take a sleeping pill. She wondered if she *had* a sleeping pill. Not that she wanted to be asleep. She just didn't want to be awake. Not now. Not till the morning. Things would look better in the morning. Like that song from *Annie*. She hated that song. So damn optimistic, you just had to be a pessimist to sing it.

She was never going to fall asleep.

Chapter

4 3

Cora's eyes snapped open. Someone was in the house. She was sure of it. Buddy wasn't barking. There was no sound, no movement, no light, except the glow from the digital clock.

Cora raised her head, took a look. 2:15. How long had she been asleep? It couldn't have been long. She thought she'd *never* fall asleep. But she must have.

Could she have dreamed it?

Cora reached for the night table, groped for her gun. She picked it up, felt an immediate sense of relief. She was *not* helpless. He was armed, and she was taking action.

Cora reached back to the night table, switched on the light.

It lit him up in bold relief. Framed in the doorway, an angel of death. He was thin and wiry, dressed all in black, some formfitting material that accentuated his muscles.

He had a stocking over his head, just as he had before. He was not holding a gun, or any other weapon. His hands were empty. And yet from his posture he seemed very much in control.

Cora pointed her gun. "Who are you?" she demanded.

He chuckled. "You don't know? It's going to eat at you that you couldn't figure it out."

It was the first time she'd heard his voice. It was not familiar, didn't help her at all.

"Oh, what fun I've had with you. Crossword puzzles. Sudoku. All the things you thrive on. What fun, beating you at your own game. Watching you chase your tail, like a stupid dog."

At her reaction, he said, "Oh, your stupid dog will be fine, by the way, as soon as he wakes up from the ether. You want a watchdog, you really could do better. Too bad you won't be around to profit from the advice."

"You're mighty cocky, considering I'm the one holding the gun."

"You're not going to shoot me. You want to know what happened. It's got to be driving you crazy. A puzzle that you can't solve."

Cora was actually glad to hear that. Whatever else the man knew, apparently he didn't know she couldn't solve crosswords.

"You're obviously too smart for me. Tell me where I went wrong."

"No. Then you'd feel free to shoot me, and I don't intend to be shot."

"What do you intend to do?"

"I thought I'd make you suffer and die. That's certainly the sequence. I mean, you can't die and then suffer."

"And just how are you going to accomplish that?"

"I'm not really sure. I've never tortured anyone before. But I did some research. Painful methods of interrogation. Not that I want you to tell me anything. That's part of the fun. Nothing you do will stop the pain."

He tapped the black leather pouch he carried on his belt. "There's enough in here to do the job. From what I've read, it should be pretty effective. Be interesting to see if what I've learned is true. There's only so much you can tell from reading. After a while you need lab experiments."

Cora started to speak, but caught herself. The man was delusional, clearly insane. And yet she didn't want to shoot him. But she would if he tried to cut her. What did he have in that bag? Scalpels? Dental equipment, like Laurence Olivier in *Marathon Man*? If he tried anything like that, she would shoot him. Cora hated going to the dentist under any circumstances. A lunatic with no novocaine was not her idea of a good time.

"Weighing your options?" he said mockingly. "You don't have any. Right now the only thing you've got going for you is I like playing with your mind. Otherwise, I could have killed you in your sleep. You do realize that, don't you? If that were the object, there was nothing to stop me. I could have smothered you with a pillow, shot you in the head, administered a lethal dose by hypodermic. No, I wanted you alive."

"Too bad the feeling isn't mutual."

"Oh, you are so good with words, aren't you? The celebrated Puzzle Lady. How well you've done all these years, with your newspaper columns and TV commercials. And number puzzles, too. There is no end to your accomplishments. I haven't been so lucky. But then, how could I, thanks to you."

He cocked his head. "No clue? I love it. 'Puzzle Lady Doesn't Have a Clue.' There's a headline for that reporter who married your niece. Well, not that headline, but I wonder if he'll write the story. He won't want to, but he'll have to. It'll be news. I wonder if anyone will figure it out. They should, but by then I'll be long gone."

He chuckled. "You're baffled. Well, guess it's time to introduce myself."

He reached up, took hold of the silk stocking, and pulled it off his head.

He was older than she'd thought, maybe forty, forty-five. His eyes were slightly sunken, and there were the beginnings of lines on his face. He was paler than she would have expected a man of his athletic build.

He grinned at her, a cocky, mocking grin. "How are you, Cora?"

She blinked. Stared at him. He seemed vaguely familiar, but she couldn't place him.

His smile faded. "Oh, my God. You don't remember me. I don't believe it. I meant so little to you, and you meant so much to me. It figures. Egocentric, self-absorbed TV personality. Why should you remember? Just because I helped launch your career."

Cora was utterly baffled. Launch her career? It was Sherry who'd launched her career—in fact, invented it, made it up out of whole cloth. That was back in the days when she was still drinking, which might explain it, if he were someone she'd met back then. There were lots of men from those days that she wouldn't remember. He could have been one of them. He'd have been a little young for her, but that never stopped her before. It would make sense if he were someone from that era.

But launch her career?

"Oh, for goodness' sakes. This is embarrassing. I'll just have to tell you. I'm Stuart Tanner."

Cora's mind was turning backflips. Stuart Tanner? She'd heard the name recently, but in what context? She had no idea. If the scene weren't so bizarre, maybe she could figure it out. But here, in the middle of the night, with an insane killer taunting her with enigmatic boasts about launching her career . . .

Cora's face froze.

Killer.

Oh, my God.

He grinned. "Ah. Finally, the penny drops. I wasn't talking about your show biz career. I meant your amateur career. I was the first killer you helped the police arrest."

It all came rushing back to her. The dead girl in the cemetery. The crossword clues. The final confrontation with this very man. The first time she'd helped Chief Harper with a case. Helped put a killer in jail. That was where she'd heard his name. Chief Harper, telling her he'd come up for parole. After only twelve years of a sentence of twenty-five to life. Harper'd assured her he wouldn't get it. Harper had been wrong. Why hadn't they alerted him? Why hadn't they alerted her? What the hell was wrong with the penal system? Letting an insane killer go, who shouldn't have been let go in the first place, and then not alerting the people he'd have reason to resent, the people he'd want to take revenge on. If she got out of this, the correctional system was going to be sorry.

Cora snorted angrily. What was she thinking, if she got out of this? She was the one with the gun.

"Yes, I know who you are, and I know what I did. I got you arrested once. Now I'm going to get you arrested again."

"I'm glad you think so."

"Oh, I know so. That's what's going to happen. Unless you force me to shoot you. Some people do that, don't they? Death by cop? I'm not a cop, but it's the same idea. You put me in a position where I have to kill you. Which is somehow very satisfying to you. Well, to each his own."

He waved his hand. "Yes, yes, yes. You're so clever with all your theories. But that's all they are. Theories. They don't work in real life. If fact, they're dead wrong. I'm not trying to get you to kill me. Quite the opposite. I'm going to kill you. Right now, the only thing in question is which way am I going to do it? The short, painless way, or the long, slow, painful way? You're going to opt for the long, slow, painful way. I know you don't believe me now, but, trust me, you will. Well, let's begin, shall we?"

He unzipped his waist bag.

Cora gestured with the gun. "Don't even think about it."

"That's all I've been doing for years. Thinking about it. Now I'm going to do it."

He reached in the bag, pulled out a gun. Small caliber, most likely a .22. From that range, Cora knew, it would be quite effective.

"The first shot is critical. Debilitating, but not fatal. That's the trick. That and leaving you fully awake."

He raised the gun, took aim.

Cora couldn't wait any longer. She pointed the gun at him, point-blank, and pulled the trigger.

The gun went click.

Chapter

44

He smiled. "Isn't that the sweetest sound in the world? A hammer clicking on an empty chamber. There's more of them, if you'd like to try again. I unloaded your gun before I woke you up. Simple precaution. I couldn't count on you to do the right thing. An impetuous person like you. Couldn't even wait to see what the right thing was. Anyway, that gun's not going to do you much good. Unless you want to throw it at me."

He held up the .22. "On the other hand, this one's fully loaded. Not that I'm going to shoot you. That is the quick-over-bang solution. That is the first option. That is door number one. If you take the first option, you will be dead. Which will be a personal disappointment to me. But at least I will get the satisfaction of knowing you take your guilt to the grave. What guilt, you might ask? Well, if you chose the short, painless option, I have to shoot you. Shooting you will wake up your niece. And her reporter husband. And that baby of hers. And then I will have to kill them. Even if the gunshot doesn't wake them, I will have to kill them. Because that's my promise to you, and I don't break my promises. So, you will die, knowing you doomed your family.

"But if you cooperate—if you allow yourself to be slowly and painfully executed—you have my word I will leave your family alone.

"So, you can be a hero, or you can be a mewling, whining, pathetic piece of humanity, sacrificing your own family to save yourself pain."

He smiled. "I'm not sure which I like more."

"If you hurt my family—"

"It will be entirely your fault. That's right. Not what you meant, I'm sure. But that's a particularly empty threat, seeing as how you're totally in my power."

Cora was hopelessly torn. Her every instinct was to fight. But could she overpower him? If she couldn't, she'd be dooming her family. And there was no reason to think she could. He was younger, stronger, he had a gun. What was she going to do? Lunge for him, dodge a bullet, choke him to death? It was the longest of long shots. Would she risk her family on that?

The answer was easy. She couldn't do it. So what was she going to do? Sit here and be tortured? She couldn't do that either. She had to stall him, fend off the moment of truth until she thought of something. If she could.

What was she talking about? If she could? She had to.

"I still don't understand," Cora said. "What you've done makes no sense. Sure, I get the whole revenge bit. But the rest of it defies logic. I mean who was that guy in New York?"

"A very unlucky man. And a very careless one. Do you know how easy it was to open his safe? I closed it and locked it, of course, so it wouldn't corroborate your story of a robber, but opening it was a snap. One picks up a lot of skills in jail. I should thank you for that. Though I'm not going to. I'm going to kill you instead."

"You say 'unlucky.' Does that mean you chose him at random?"

"I had to stage a crime to set you up."

"Yeah, but why him?"

"It had to be someone. He filled the bill."

"How did you choose him?"

Tanner waved the question away impatiently. "That's not important."

"Well, what about the town clerk? That made no sense at all."

"Part of the puzzle."

"Yeah, but why her? And why break into Town Hall? I'm assuming that was you. What could you possibly hope to accomplish?"

"I'm not sure I should tell you. I wouldn't want you to think poorly of me."

"Right," Cora said sarcastically. "I thought it didn't matter what I think. Because I'm going to be dead."

"Good point. Even so, I'd like you to admire my cunning. All right, I'll tell you. You built an addition on your house."

Cora blinked. "What?"

He grinned. "Telling you isn't so bad after all. To see you baffled like that. Well worth it. But that's the answer. You built an addition on your house. Can you think how that might motivate my actions? You can't, can you? Well, my little failing doesn't seem so bad now, does it? I'll have to spell it out for you. You substantially altered the look of your house. It is now unrecognizable from the road. And the fact is, I forgot your address. I couldn't find it. And it's unlisted. Your address, your phone number, everything. From when your niece was hiding out from her husband. Not the reporter, her first husband."

He shrugged, smiled. "The problem is, I'm a convicted killer. And if I'm gonna kill someone else, I can't come walking into town and ask where they live. When they put together the killer's dos and don'ts list, guess which one was near the top? I managed to bundle up so I was almost unrecognizable, drop into Town Hall, and tell the town clerk, whom I had never met, that I was thinking about buying a small house in Bakerhaven with a view toward expanding it, but I was concerned about zoning ordinances, and could she show me any recent additions that had been approved for expansion in the last few years, particularly any ranch house being expanded into a two-family dwelling. I'd have got the address, plus the layout of the house to facilitate the current situation. Knowing all their bedrooms were upstairs, for instance.

"But, no, little Miss Starchy-Bottom parrots rules at me. Of course it's against the rules, but a human being cuts you a break. Anyway, she wouldn't budge an inch, so I had to break in and see for myself. Which is what elevated the useless bimbo into the role of Victim Number Two. That and the danger the lamebrain might eventually associate the guy asking about building addition blueprints with the murder."

Cora frowned. "How is that connected with the murder?"

"Not *his* murder. *Your* murder. When your body turns up in a recently expanded ranch house. It might give her cause to think. Probably not, but hey, I needed a victim anyway."

"Okay, I understand you harassing me. But why leave a crossword puzzle at Crowley's house?"

"You and the sergeant had been getting far too cozy. I just had to break you up." He frowned. "You're not asking for information. You're just stalling for time. Well, guess what? You're out of time. Time to play the game."

Crowley reached in his waist bag, took out a silencer, and screwed it on the end of the automatic.

"See, I keep my word. As long as you keep yours, this is just between us. If you stop cooperating, I kill your niece. And her husband. And her daughter. I go straight upstairs, bang, over, dead. I disable you so you can't walk, I pull that phone cord out of the wall, I go upstairs and I kill them all. Is that what you want?"

"No."

"So let's get on with it. I know what I have to shoot in order to disable you. I just may not be able to hit it."

Tanner raised the gun, pointed it at Cora.

Crowley stepped in the door and shot him in the back.

Crowley handcuffed Tanner's hands together behind his back, and dumped him unceremoniously facedown on the floor. Tanner never made a sound.

"You shot him," Cora said.

Crowley shrugged. "You don't shoot a bad guy now and then, you get rusty."

"How many bad guys have you shot?"

"All right, you got me. He's my first one."

"You were there the whole time?"

"I saw him go in."

"You couldn't have stepped in sooner?"

"Why? He seemed like the type of guy who might have confessed."

"Or shot me in the head."

Crowley shrugged. "It was touch and go when he picked up your gun. When he dumped out the bullets, I figured him for the chatty sort. And I didn't want to get him for breaking and entering. Without his confession, that's all we had. I mean, can I prove he did everything else? I can *infer* it. But unless he's carrying the murder weapon . . . And he's not. We may not have been able to match up the fatal bullet, but it certainly wasn't a twenty-two. And until he started talking, I had no idea who he was. If I'd known he was an ex-con with a grudge—"

Tanner moaned. Pulled against the cuffs.

"Sounds like he's coming to," Cora said.

"Yeah. Wanna hit him with something?"

Cora gave him a look.

Crowley put up his hands. "Sorry. Cop talk, while waiting for the EMS. I keep forgetting you're a civilian."

"Among other things," Cora said.

Crowley shifted his eyes. He seemed on the verge of saying something, but Aaron poked his head in the door.

"Sherry thought she heard a shot." His eyes widened. "Oh, my God, she did."

"It's okay, we got the killer," Crowley said. "The cops are on the way."

Aaron blinked bleary eyes at him. "Cora said you weren't here."

"That was just a bluff to make the killer overconfident."

"You shot him?"

"He was going to shoot Cora. He's lucky I didn't kill him. Go tell your wife it's okay."

Aaron went out.

Crowley turned back to Cora. He didn't seem to know how to begin. He opened his mouth.

There came the sound of tires on gravel in the driveway.

Cora frowned, but Crowley looked like he'd gotten a reprieve from the governor.

"Guess the cops are here," Cora said.

But it was Barney Nathan.

"You're early, Barney," Cora said. "He's not dead yet."

"The hospital called me," Barney said. "Some delay with EMS." But he couldn't look at her, and seemed uncomfortable to be there.

In spite of everything, Cora was amused. It was a strange dynamic, her two lovers there together. Barney didn't have a clue about the situation, but Cora was sure Crowley picked up on it. The doctor was so stiff and formal and self-conscious, there could be only one explanation.

Barney knelt by the prisoner, clung to his task like a lifeline. He popped open his medical bag, took out a surgical scissors, and cut the black turtleneck away. He pressed sterile gauze pads to the wound, stemmed the flow of blood.

"How is he?" Cora said.

"He'll live."

"Too bad."

Barney looked at her sharply but said nothing, turned his attention back to the wound.

Another sound of gravel from the driveway proved to be the EMS unit. Barney turned the patient over to them gratefully, but before he could make his escape, Harper arrived, followed closely by Dan Finley. The officers wanted the story, and mistakenly thought Barney was a source of information.

While Crowley was attempting to explain, Sherry arrived in her bathrobe and wanted him to start over.

Barney managed to slip away during the confusion, but Chief Harper wouldn't let the EMS unit take the prisoner, since he was under arrest. Harper placed him in Dan Finley's custody, relieving Crowley of the responsibility. Cora hoped that would mean Crowley could stay behind. Unfortunately, he had shot the prisoner, so he had to go down to the station to file a report. Dan Finley tagged along to handcuff him to the hospital bed.

By the time they all left, Cora was ready to collapse, but Sherry wanted to know what happened. Cora couldn't blow her off. She had to tell her.

Leaving certain things out.

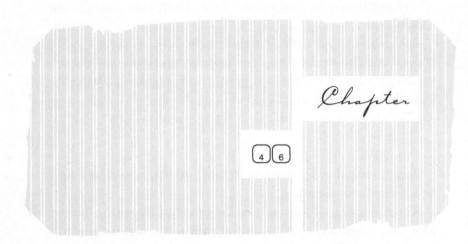

Chapter 46

Chief Harper hung up the phone and turned to Crowley and Cora, who were studiously avoiding each other almost as self-consciously as Barney Nathan had avoided Cora the night before.

Harper didn't notice. "Well, I think that wraps it up," he said. "Tanner's on his way back to County to serve out his sentence for violating his parole. A couple of new murder charges are just the icing on the cake. The question is whether we can make 'em stick."

"I should think so," Cora said. "He confessed the whole thing to me."

"That's hearsay."

"I believe it's an admission against interest. You might wanna check with Ratface."

"I'm not so sure about that," Harper said. "You're a suspect in the investigation." He jerked his thumb at Crowley. "He's the guy who shot him. You throw out what you 'impartial witnesses' heard, and what have we got."

"I imagine if you ask around, you can get some corroboration," Cora said.

"How?"

"Get some prisoner to snitch. How did Tanner pick his first victim? It'll turn out some prisoner told him about this wealthy schmuck with a wall-safe a child could get into. Or it will turn out Tanner knew him before. Was familiar with the layout of his apartment. That one I like, because he knew he could jump out the window and land on the balcony rather than fall fourteen stories straight down. And he knew he could get by the front desk and get upstairs."

"How?"

"How the hell should I know? There's a back door to the basement that's always unlocked. He noticed when he was helping the guy get something out of the storeroom. Or something like that. If you look, you'll find it, because it has to be there, because he didn't go by the front desk. Frankly, I like the prisoner told him about the easy mark. Because he's going back to jail, where the prisoner who told him will be pissed he killed the easy mark. Anyway, he picked him, and lured me up there to find the body.

"He devised this scheme. He had years to do it. It was an obsession. He taught himself how to do crossword puzzles. He taught himself how to do sudoku. He hatched a diabolical plot where crossword puzzle clues would lead me on a merry chase, getting me deeper and deeper in trouble myself, starting with a murder that I not only couldn't solve, but looked like the prime suspect. He called Becky Baldwin, said he was Charles Kessington and he wanted to hire her, and lured her up to his apartment."

"How did he know you'd come along?"

"He's been following my cases in the papers. He knew Becky'd been hiring me lately. He deliberately put her in a position where she wouldn't want to come alone. Insisting on meeting her in his bachelor penthouse. He knew she'd bring me, and he knew I'd have a gun. If he could get me to fire it, it would be perfect.

"Anyway, he gets there, kills the guy, and waits for me to arrive. I do, he makes a sound in the bedroom, and I come in with gun drawn. He turns, dives out the window. He jumps up with his gun, and pretends to shoot me. Naturally, I fire. As expected, the shot goes out the window. He runs along the balcony, over the roof, and out the escape route he planned, leaving me with a corpse and a fired gun just in time for the cops to rush in and arrest me."

"And the town clerk?"

"I told you. He broke into town hall to get my address. He killed the town clerk for being a pain in the ass about it, and because he was afraid after I got killed she might remember him coming around asking questions."

"Why did he need your address? Couldn't he just follow you home?"

"He did, but it was after the first murder. That was the only time he knew where I was, and the only time he could follow me through Bakerhaven without fear of being spotted. He hung around the crime scene, followed when the police ran me in. He waited outside for Becky to spring me—he knew she would—and followed us to the garage to get our car. It must have been a kick in the chops when we went to a play instead of going home. But he hung around the theater until the play was over, waited while we got our car out of yet another garage, and followed us to Bakerhaven. Both to find out where I lived, and to make me nervous. He let us spot him a couple of times, and get his license plate, the bogus one that didn't exist in any motor vehicle records, but showed up in the sudoku."

"I suppose."

"Hey, you don't like it, tough noogies. I'm the one got a gun pulled in my face and threatened with torture tactics."

Harper turned to Crowley. "All right, I understand why he was hassling her. Why was he hassling you?"

Crowley looked embarrassed.

Cora jumped in with, "Guilt by association. He was my

arresting officer. He was bringing the puzzles to me. When we went to Penn Station to retrieve the clue in the lockers, Tanner was undoubtedly watching."

"Yeah, but he said 'friend.' 'Any friend of my enemy may offend.'"

Cora smiled. "I always think kindly of my arresting officers."

Chapter

4 7

Crowley and Cora came out of the police station and walked to his car parked down the block.

Crowley turned back. "Look, I want to say something."

"I'm sure you do. You just can't find the words."

"I'm no good at this."

"No kidding."

"You're not making this easy on me."

"Any reason why I should?"

"I deserve that, I know. I'm just trying to tell you how it is."

"How is it?"

Crowley took a breath. "Yes, I have a long-standing relationship with that girl. Occasionally we get together. For long stretches we don't. We've both had other relationships. When we do, that's fine. When they've run their course, well, we're always there."

"And this has run its course."

"I didn't say that."

"You didn't have to. I understand. I'm yesterday's news."

"You're no such thing. I don't know what you are. You're the most remarkable woman I've ever met."

"What girl doesn't want to hear that."

"Oh, for God's sake. We were fine until that son of a bitch screwed it up. *He* screwed it up. He *meant* to screw it up. He did it deliberately. That's why he left the puzzle at my ex-wife's house."

Cora opened her mouth.

"Yes, I said 'ex-wife.' You want me to call her my wife? She hasn't been that in fifteen years. What's legal's not important."

"Sort of a strange position for a cop."

Crowley smiled ruefully. "I knew it the minute I said it. You know what I mean. The thing is, it's a shame to let him win."

"Oh, you sweet-talking man. Be still my heart."

The early-morning Bakerhaven street was bustling. Cora couldn't remember it so crowded. Or maybe she'd never tried to have a personal conversation outside the police station before. But she'd become increasingly aware of people around her. On the sidewalk in front of Cushman's Bake Shop, the usual crowd was hanging out, including young mothers with strollers. She was glad Sherry wasn't among them. That would be more that she could bear.

But there were people she knew. First Selectman Iris Cooper, for instance, waved to her. Cora didn't want to be outwardly rude, but she didn't want to invite Iris over. Her answering wave was as discouraging as possible.

Cora turned back to Crowley. "You're saying nothing happened?"

"What do you mean, 'happened'?"

"You're saying you want to go on as before."

"Well, you gotta understand," Crowley said. He broke off, grimaced.

"I get it," Cora said. "You live in the city. I live in the town. The case is over. There's no reason for us to see each other anymore. You gotta get back to work. You have other cases. Even if you don't have other women. Which you may, but giving you the benefit of the doubt."

"Cora . . ."

"That's the situation, isn't it? I don't mean the other women. I mean the getting back to work. It's like you said, our relationship has run its course. The polite thing to do is say good-bye. Maybe we'll see each other again someday, and maybe we won't. Forcing it now would be one of those big mistakes people make when they think they're doing the right thing. And they're doing it for all the wrong reasons and they resent it, so they wind up resenting each other. And on and on down the slippery slope to divorce. Only we're lucky. We don't need a divorce. We can simply shake hands and walk away."

Cora wanted very much to do that, because she couldn't keep the conversation going without breaking down, making an unseemly public display of herself.

The scene was getting more public by the minute. Dan Finley had driven up, and Chief Harper had come out the front door to meet him. They stood on the sidewalk talking.

While Cora watched, Dr. Barney Nathan came out of Cushman's Bake Shop holding a latte and a scone.

Cora couldn't take it. She turned back to Crowley, held out her hand. "So," she said. "I guess this is good-bye."

Crowley looked at her hand, but he didn't take it. He looked back up at her.

"Aw, hell," Crowley said.

He took her in his arms, and kissed her in front of half the town.